JAMES P. BLAYLOCK

The Affair
of the
Chalk Cliffs

The Affair
of the
Chalk Cliffs

JAMES P. BLAYLOCK

Illustrated by J. K. Potter

SUBTERRANEAN PRESS 2011

First Edition

ISBN
978-1-59606-365-5

Subterranean Press
PO Box 190106
Burton, MI 48519

www.subterraneanpress.com

Chapter 1

Madness at the
Explorers Club

THE MOOD AROUND THE table at the Half Toad Inn, Lambert Court, that Saturday evening in spring was lamentable, despite the food, which consisted of an enormous steak and kidney pie that Henrietta Billson had five minutes earlier drawn forth from the oven and set out steaming on the table in front of Professor Langdon St. Ives, his man Hasbro, and myself—Jack Owlesby. There were grilled oysters, tidbits of cold mackerel dusted with salt, roasted potatoes and potted leeks. Dead center of the table stood a gallon of Olde Man Newt, William Billson's own ale, served at the Half Toad in wide-mouthed vessels. Mrs. Billson was just then turning a jam roly-poly on a floured board, which would be hot out of the oven in half an hour. It might be said that she looked like some variety of roly-poly herself, although it would be an insult to the woman, and so I won't say it. A half hour earlier she threatened to run a man out of the inn who hadn't any manners but was "all swank talk," and when the man said something clever to her she bent his arm up behind his neck, kicked him half a dozen times in the seat of his pants, and drove him head foremost out the door.

Now rain hammered at the windows along Fingal Street on this stay-at-home evening, the room nearly empty although there was surely no better place to be in Greater London. There were oysters on the plate and ale in the glass, but a morose Langdon St. Ives apparently tasted nothing, stabbing at the bivalves with an indifferent fork and borne down by the blue devils. St. Ives, as perhaps you might already know, is the greatest, if largely unheralded, explorer and scientist in the Western World. I know little of scientists in the Eastern World, where there might well be some Mandarin equivalent of Professor St. Ives piecing together a magnetic engine for a voyage to the moon, a chronicler like myself peering over his shoulder, sharpening a nib and rustling foolscap. But St. Ives's stature as a man of science meant nothing to him tonight, and Hasbro's subtle efforts to interest him in a slice of mackerel went unheeded; he might as well have been sitting in a cell in the Fleet Prison staring at a plate of salted oakum.

We had just that afternoon returned from Scotland, from Dundee on the Firth of Tay, where the Rail Bridge had collapsed into the firth in December of last year, three days after Christmas, taking a train with it along with seventy-five passengers. St. Ives had been a boyhood friend of Sir Thomas Bouch in Cumbria in the first half of the century, and Bouch, as you no doubt recall, was vilified by the courts and in the press for having badly engineered the bridge. St. Ives had received a letter from Bouch, imploring his help, and we had gone up to Dundee to discover whether deviltry was the cause of the collapse as much as shoddy workmanship. The submarine vessel of the infamous Dr. Ignacio Narbondo had reportedly been sighted on several occasions in the firth during that fateful month of December. By the time we arrived, however, Bouch had decamped to Glasgow, and we were left to our own devices, pursuing our suspicions up half-blind avenues that came to nothing. The authorities declared St. Ives's suspicions about Narbondo's machinations to be fantastic, worthy of the imagination of Mr. Jules Verne.

When we ran Bouch to ground in Glasgow, he had no idea that we were in Scotland. He hadn't sent any letter to St. Ives or to anyone else, and he had never heard of Dr. Ignacio Narbondo.

If our failure to forestall the ruin of Sir Thomas Bouch were the long and the short of it, the food and drink and the comforts of the Half Toad might have fetched the home stake, as the Americans say, but St. Ives was further diminished by a recent falling out with Alice, Mrs. St. Ives, who had grown weary of her husband's constant adventures. He had promised her a month-long holiday on Lake Windermere, before the summer crowds descended, but fast on the heels of his solemn promise had come word from Scotland. Honor left St. Ives no choice but to set out for Dundee to help his old friend, the holiday abandoned. Alice, you understand, agreed that St. Ives must undertake the journey, but she wasn't happy about it, and they had parted ways in cold silence, St. Ives to Scotland and Alice to Heathfield in East Sussex to visit her niece Sydnee. This silence between her and St. Ives had lasted close upon two weeks now, and St. Ives had been deafened by it, the sun having utterly disappeared from the cloudy firmament of his soul.

Alice is a sort of paragon of wives, equally handy with a fowling piece or a fishing rod, and can quote Izaak Walton six to the dozen, as if she has the *Angler* by memory. She's as competent as Henrietta Billson to kick a man in his daily duty if he asks for it, and pardon the expression. Although the particulars of their marriage are none of my business, I'll insist that she understands

St. Ives fully, and has looked with equanimity on giant squids autopsied in the larder and pygmy hippopotami occupying the barn. (A canal for the hippopotami was, I'll admit, a recurring subject of contention.) In short, she's the perfect mate for a scientist and adventurer like St. Ives. But the man's zealous sense of duty to the world and to science, admirable as it is, could try the patience of a marble saint.

St. Ives gazed at his kidney pie, nodding senselessly at our efforts to rally him, tasting his drink and setting the glass down again. Nothing useful could be done this side of Alice's homecoming. She was due into Victoria Station tonight at half past nine o'clock.

The door opened and our old friend Tubby Frobisher staggered in out of the weather, oddly taking no notice of us there in the corner. He attempted to hang up a dripping coat and hat before heading across to warm his considerable bulk at the fire, but the coat fell to the floor and the hat on top of it. I nodded to Lars Hopeful, Billson's halfwit tap boy, who fetched the garments from the floor and hung them up near enough to the fire to roast them. Tubby's usual cheerful demeanor had abdicated. He looked like a man pursued by demons, his rotund face haggard, his eyes wild, his hair apparently coifed by the Barber of Seville, who, of course, had been dead these two centuries past. His clothing was askew as well, his shirt yanked half out of his trousers, his right sleeve gaping open.

He spotted that roly-poly pudding just going into the oven, a sight that would normally lend him the giddy look of a hedgehog eyeing a worm, but he turned away as if blind to it. Then he saw the three of us sitting at our table and seemed to recall, from deep within his mind, that he had in fact agreed to meet us at just that hour—that he had no doubt come to the Half Toad for that very reason. He veered toward us now, laboring like a dockyard lump in a side wind, sitting down heavily in a chair, where he gaped and blinked.

"What cheer, Tubby?" I said to him, but he looked at me as if I'd uttered an insult. Then, coming to himself at last, he picked up my glass and drained half a pint of Olde Man Newt in a single draught.

"I've just come from the Explorer's Club," he said, shaking his head darkly and setting the glass down hard. His face was plowed with deep furrows, and he gave us a look that was heavy with meaning, although I was damned if I could make it out. St. Ives sat deathly still, not so much as acknowledging Tubby's pronouncement, his own mind still traveling in a dark country. I signaled Hopeful to bring along another glass, since Tubby had seized upon mine. "I believe that I momentarily witnessed the end of civilization," Tubby muttered.

"I trust that you comported yourself with dignity," I said to him, filling both our glasses from the pitcher.

"I did not," he told me, evidently serious. "Dignity wasn't in it. It was the most extraordinary thing. The strangest turn of events."

"More extraordinary even than dignity?" I asked. "Pray tell us what happened. The champagne ran short? Duel in the bookroom?"

"I'll tell you what it was," he said, "although I still doubt myself. I went out of my mind, quite literally, and when I stepped back into it I found that I had taken a cutlass off the wall and hacked the head from that stuffed boar in among the potted plants by the gallery window. I was dead certain that it was attacking me, and I laid it out with a single stroke. I vaguely recall singing "The Sorrows of Old Bailey," looking down at the decapitated monster and wondering why it didn't bleed. I admired that boar. Attacking it was unconscionable."

"Tubby Frobisher *singing*? That's bad, very bad," I told him. "Whisky might account for it."

"Whisky be damned!" he shouted, glowering at me. "I'd had nothing but a cup of hot punch. There was *no* accounting for it—that's what I'm telling you, confound it. The entire *room* was in the same straits. Lord Kelvin was smoking three clay pipes at once while balanced on one leg atop a divan, and that French somnambulist whose name never fails to escape me was setting in to shoot the pipe out of his mouth with a pistol. He had already blasted a vase full of crocuses to smithereens. Secretary Parsons was accusing some harmless old blighter of being the Devil, shouting that he would cut out his liver and lights with a sharpened spoon. You've never seen such a thing—utter chaos and uproar. Every man a raving lunatic, living geniuses reeling and chattering like gibbon apes."

Tubby had grown red in the face, half bonkers again simply recalling the scene. I could see that he was deadly serious, but even so I was again on the point of saying something droll when I noticed that St. Ives had awakened from his deep stupor.

"You say that every man jack of you went mad?" he asked. *"At the same instant?"*

"That's just what I say, Professor. Tomorrow it'll be in the news. No way to keep it quiet, what with Admiral Peavey pitching furniture off the balcony and shouting at people on the street below to clear the buggering decks. Bedlam reigned. Utterly scandalous behavior for two or three minutes. Then the spell lifted like a curtain and we were all of us left gaping at each other, begging pardon right and left." Tubby gobbled three oysters in rapid succession, washed them down with the ale, and then carved out a piece of kidney pie. "God bless an oyster," he said, heaving a great sigh.

"And the people in the street—they were unaffected by this...fit?" St. Ives asked, his eyes alive for the first time in two days.

"I can't quite say," Tubby told him. "There was no sign to the contrary aside from a general uproar, but perhaps that had something to do with the flying chairs."

"You mentioned that cup of punch," Hasbro put in, speaking in his customary, even tone, as if Tubby had been talking about the price of wool. "I wonder whether someone hadn't put a chemical into it. May I attend to your shirt cuff, sir?" Tubby noticed then that he was dragging his unlatched cuff through the mackerel, and he allowed Hasbro to swab it with a napkin and button it up. He took stock of himself then, and made a belated effort to smooth down his hair with a dab of fish oil.

As I said earlier, Hasbro is St. Ives's manservant, his factotum. They'd been comrades in arms time out of mind, and had traveled together to destinations that beggar description. Hasbro has saved St. Ives's life more than once, and St. Ives has returned the favor. He's a tall man, Hasbro is, well turned out, with a long face and a demeanor that rarely changes its atmosphere. He's a crack shot with a pistol, and I've seen him reef and steer as if he were Poseidon's nephew. His notions about punch and poison were sensible. Everything about the man was sensible.

"Poisoning might explain it," St. Ives said, although he didn't seem convinced. "Lord knows what it would be, given that the effects were transitory and apparently immediate. Some variety of plant extract, perhaps. Datura might do the trick, in the form of a condensed tea brewed from the roots. But what would account for the sudden cessation of effect? Dosage? Surely everyone hadn't consumed the same quantity, and of course no two men are constructed alike." He forked up a dripping lump of kidney and seemed to eat it almost happily now, his mind revolving on the trouble at hand rather than the trouble soon to be awaiting him at Victoria Station.

"But *all* of us?" Tubby said. *"The staff as well?"*

"Who's to say the staff hadn't been lapping up the punch?" I asked. "They're not immune to the attraction of warm spirits on a cold evening. For my money Hasbro has put his finger on it. The mystery is solved."

"*Half* the mystery, perhaps, even if it is the case," St. Ives said. "The other half is the more vital."

"Which other half?" I asked.

"Whose hand is behind the outrage, and, of course, why?"

He seemed to grow distracted, as if something had come into his mind, and he cocked his head curiously. For a moment I waited for him to advance some further, enlightening theory, but the clock spoke the hour, and we set in to eat in earnest, time being short. With food going down his gullet Tubby seemed to have forgotten his embarrassment, and agreed with me that he had been fortunate to hack the head off a stuffed boar rather than off the shoulders of Admiral Peavey. After the third glass of ale he was laughing about the entire business, brandishing his stick and insisting that I act the part of the boar for the general amusement of Billson's patronage. I declined. Mrs. Billson set the roly-poly pudding on the table and sliced it, the currant jam leaking out in a purple river, and it seemed to me that all our troubles could be put right by a kidney pie, a pudding, and a pint of ale.

Chapter 2

The Commercial Traveler

TEN MINUTES LATER WE went out into the rainy night beneath umbrellas, considerably improved in spirit, although soon St. Ives fell into an anxious silence again, the awful moment approaching. Hasbro and Tubby walked on ahead, which gave me an opportunity to say something useful to my friend. "Throw yourself on the mercy of the court," I told him. "That's the smoothest path when it comes to making up with wives. Fewer thorns and clinkers if you take that route. I can't claim experience, but I've read widely on the topic. Common sense supports my argument."

"I intend to do just that," he said. He walked along in silence for a time, and then said, "If Alice will have me back, I'll…"

"Don't talk rubbish," I said, emboldened, perhaps, by that pudding. "Have you back from *where*? She hasn't sent you away."

"Not yet she hasn't," he said with sad defeat in his voice. "Not yet."

"Then pray do not compound the problem by anticipating any such thing. Pardon my saying so, but you sell her short. Thinking evil sometimes invites it, and the opposite, too. I suggest that you start by assuming on Alice's better nature, and your own, for that matter. You couldn't simply leave Bouch to twist in the wind, after all. Alice knows that."

He gave me a long stare and then nodded his head. "You're in the right of it," he said, "although that's precisely what came of our ill-fated trip to Dundee. I'll beg her forgiveness, though, and then steel myself for the onslaught. Perhaps it won't come. We don't deserve them, you know."

"Wives, you mean?"

"Yes. Few men are worthy of the women they marry."

"Tell her just that thing. Give her a chance to agree with you. That should cheer her up immensely."

We continued in that vein of chat for some time, oblivious to the activities roundabout, until we were vaguely surprised to find ourselves on Victoria Street, the broad arch of the great railway station looming before us. Coaches and dogcarts clogged the boulevard, and rattled away in either direction, and there was a great noise of people coming out of the station and going in, the entryway illuminated by gas lamps flickering in the damp wind. We still had our umbrellas hoisted, although the rain had mostly stopped without our realizing it. I can't imagine that I had said anything to St. Ives that was worth more than two shillings, but perhaps I had distracted him from himself, which was something.

Hasbro and Tubby had already entered the station, and we steeled ourselves and walked into the bustle and clamor of the crowds, the hissing of locomotives, and the smell of wet wool and engine oil. The hour had come, and Alice's train along with it, rolling slowly into the station at that very moment, its journey at an end. The doors opened, and people descended to the platform, scores of people, from Croydon and Tunbridge Wells and points south, making their way out toward the street past heaps of luggage. For the space of some several minutes we were certain that Alice would momentarily appear among them. Then the crowd dwindled, and the platform cleared. For a time there was no one, until one last harried passenger got off—a commercial traveler by the look of him—carrying a portmanteau and with a head like a pumpkin and eyes like poached eggs. That was the end of the exodus. No Alice.

"Gents," the commercial traveler said to us when he hove alongside and dropped anchor, "I'm in the timepiece line." He took his portmanteau in both hands and shook it, four metal legs telescoping from the bottom. A hidden drawer sprang out, revealing a velvet-lined compartment full of tolerably dusty and tarnished pocket watches. He smiled in a toothy and unconvincing way, his shop set up on the instant and open for business.

St. Ives had fully expected something unpleasant this night—longed for it, even—but Alice's non-arrival was beyond his ken. He stood blinking, completely at sea, loosed from his moorings and apparently unaware that the timepiece salesman stood before him, wearing worn tweeds and grinning into his face. Tubby was not unaware of the man's presence, however, and he said, "Shove off, mate," in a tone calculated to be understood.

"Of course," the man said. "I can see you gents are preoccupied. I… Say!" he said, suddenly bending forward and gaping at the professor. "Ain't you that chap St. Vitus? Wait! That isn't it! St. Ives! I knew I'd get it! I had the good fortune of perusing your likeness in *The Graphic*, sir, some months back. Story about a sort of enormous skeleton…? On the riverbank, I believe it was, out in Germany. I'm honored, sir." He thrust out his hand, looking admiringly at St. Ives. Then, slowly, his visage took on the air of commiseration. "Asking your pardon, sir," he said, more quietly now, "but you ain't waiting for a *Heathfield* traveler, are you? You look worn down by care, as they say."

"What do you know of Heathfield travelers?" I asked him. I'll admit that I didn't like the look of him, although I myself had written the account published in *The Graphic* concerning our exploratory trip down the Danube the previous year, from which we had returned with a giant human femur and a lower jaw set with teeth the size of dominoes. At least our watch salesman had the good sense to have read the piece.

"Only that there weren't no Heathfield travelers aboard, mate," he said in my direction. "Not tonight there weren't. The train went past Heathfield like a racehorse. Scarcely slowed down."

"Why would it do such a thing?" Tubby asked. "Damned strange behavior for a train."

The man hesitated for a moment, and then looked around conspiratorially. "They're keeping it on the quiet," he said in a low voice. "Mum's the word down south, don't you see? Some sort of *contagion*, apparently."

He had St. Ives's attention now. "Contagion?" the Professor asked. "What variety?"

"I don't know the particulars," he said. "But I'll tell you that in my way of business I talk to some…interesting people, so to say. And one of these people let on

that the village was one great Bedlam, the entire pop-
ulation picking straws out of their hair and crawling
about on their hands and knees. Madness by the buck-
etful. Mayhem in the streets. I wouldn't have stopped
in Heathfield for anything for fear of getting a dose of
it. And mark my words, now that I know what I know,
tomorrow morning I'm going back home to Hastings,
and you can be certain it'll be by way of Maidstone, and
not Tunbridge Wells."

St. Ives seemed to reel at the news, and Hasbro put
a supportive hand on his arm. We all gave each other a
look, what with Tubby's story of the recent horror at the
Explorers Club still fresh in our minds.

Wait!" the man said. "Don't tell me you've got a loved
one in Heathfield, sir?"

"His own wife," Tubby said.

"Good Lord, sir! You'd best get her out, and no delay."

"Anything more you could tell us, then?" Hasbro
asked him, keen for information.

"Well, sir," the man said, dropping his voice again,
"you didn't hear it from me. But seeing as who you are,
and that you're worried for your poor wife, and rightly
so, I'll be straight with you. Like I said, the village is
closed down tight—roads blocked, soldiers patrolling. If
you go down that way by rail, as perhaps you must, you'd
best get off at Uckfield and make your way to the village

at Blackboys. This chap I know, my sister's gentleman friend, I'm ashamed to say, who does some work in the sneak thief and housebreaking line when he ain't poaching, reckons that a man could find his way into Heathfield through the forest—past the coal fire pits alongside of Blackboys there. It's easy pickings in Heathfield with the village in an uproar, is what he told me. 'In through the front door and out again with the swag'—them was his very words. You'll say I should have him jailed, of course, given what I know, but that's not my way. What a man tells me in confidence is just that, if you understand me. Now, do you know the open country around Blackboys?"

"Tolerably well, yes," Tubby put in. "I've got an uncle in the smelting way at the Buxted Foundry. Produces railway steel for the Cuckoo Line. He's got a house there in Dicker. I've hunted my share of grouse in and about Blackboys."

"Then you know something of the place." He nodded, as if relieved to hear it.

"Why would this…acquaintance of yours chance going into the village at all?" I asked skeptically. "Never mind the authorities, it's the contagion I'm thinking of."

"It's a brain fever, you see. This fellow I'm talking about has fixed himself a cap out of those great heavy gloves they wear at the kilns. Lined with woven asbestos, they are—*amianthus* some call it. Split open and pulled down over the ears, it'll keep out the lunacy molecules like leather keeps out the wind. If you're in the mood to go into Heathfield, he's the fellow you'll be wanting to see down in Blackboys. People call him the Tipper. He's a small man, not above so." He held his hand waist high. The man was apparently a dwarf. "He's not unacquainted with the Old Coach Inn, there on the High Street. If you look him up, tell him you're a friend of Peddler Sam Burke. Give him this." He dipped into a pocket in his coat then and pulled out a card with his name on it: "Sam 'the Peddler' Burke: Watches, Jewelry, and Pawn."

And with that he once again became the man "in the timepiece line." He said loudly, "No one fancies a pocket watch, then? Very fine works. Austrian made." But he was already folding up the portmanteau, knocking the legs back in, having lost interest in us. He walked off toward the ticket counter without looking back.

"My God!" St. Ives muttered, knuckling his brow. "Here it is again. Madness springing up like a plague."

Tubby gave me a hard look. "Poisoned punch, forsooth!" he said.

"Should we send to the Half Toad for our bags, sir?" Hasbro asked St. Ives, who nodded decisively.

"If you'd like another hand," Tubby said to Hasbro, "I'm your man. I know the way of things down there, and I've always got a bag packed and ready. I'll bring my blackthorn stick, if you follow me."

"A generous offer, Sir. There's a late train south—an hour from now, I believe."

"I'll need half that," Tubby said over his shoulder, already hurrying toward the street, bowling through the slow-footed like a juggernaut.

"I'll fetch the tickets," I said, and went along in the direction taken by the Peddler, who had apparently purchased his own return ticket and gone about his business by then. I'll admit that I wouldn't have given him two shillings for one of his "Austrian-made" time-pieces. His consorting with thieves didn't recommend him, either.

The man behind the glass sat on a high stool, reading a newspaper. He glanced up at me without expression. "I'm looking for a gent," I told him, the idea coming into my mind at that very moment. "He might have got off the last train. Large, round head, sandy hair, red-faced. He generally dresses in oatmeal tweed, perhaps a little on the shabby side. He might have tried to sell you a pocket watch before buying a ticket to Hastings."

"You're three minutes late," he told me. "Your man's out on the street by now. And you mean Eastbourne, and not Hastings. He bought a ticket on tonight's train, the Beachy Head Runner."

"Beachy Head?" I said stupidly. *"Tonight's train?"* He scowled just a little, as if I'd accused him of a lie, and so I sensibly let the matter drop. Perhaps the Peddler had meant Eastbourne by way of Hastings. Perhaps he meant anything at all. Probably he was the fabulous liar of the world, about as genuine as his timepieces.

An hour later the four of us were bound for East Sussex on the very train that the Peddler himself had bought a ticket for, although I hadn't seen him board. Good riddance to bad rubbish, I thought. In Eridge we would abandon our train for a seat on the aptly named Cuckoo Line, into Uckfield, where we'd strike out overland on foot toward Blackboys if it was too late to hire a coach. With any luck, the mysterious contagion would evaporate, as it evidently had at the Explorers Club, and our sojourn would amount to nothing more than wasted hours.

I was deeply asleep, my head bumping against the window, before we were out of London.

—⁓—

WHEN I CAME awake in the dim coach, we were sitting dead still, the night outside dark and lonesome. For a moment I had no idea where I was or what I was doing there, but the sight of my sleeping companions brought me to my senses, and I sat in the lovely silence for a time and gazed out the window. I saw that I was looking out on a heath, and I could distinguish a line of trees in the distance, and a star or two in the sky, which was full of scudding clouds.

It came into my mind that I'd soon have to find the necessary room, which was situated aft. I arose quietly and made my way down the aisle, passing into the darkness at the back of the car, and trailing one hand along the wall to steady myself, expecting at any moment that the train would start forward and pitch me onto the floor. Abruptly I ran out of wall, and my hand fell away into a void. I lurched sideways, temporarily off balance, and at once heard a shuffling noise and was abruptly aware that someone—a shadow—was standing near me, hidden by the darkness. A hand gripped my arm, I was pushed sideways so that I spun half around, and before it came into my mind to cry out, I was knocked senseless.

Chapter 3

The Journey South

JACKIE!" A VOICE SAID, sounding distant and dreamlike. It occurred to me that the name was my own, or had been in some dim, earlier life. Soon after I recalled that I had eyes, and I opened them and squinted up into the worried face of Tubby Frobisher, who looked down at me, holding his blackthorn stick in his hand. My first thought was that Tubby had beaten me with it, but on second thought it seemed moderately unlikely. The train was moving along now, slowly picking up speed.

"I knocked the bugger sideways," Tubby said to me. "Broke his wrist for him, I warrant you. But he leapt out the carriage door straightaway and disappeared. A railway thief, no doubt. The man had his weapon raised to strike you again, by God, but I put an end to his filthy caper."

I managed to sit up now, but reeled back against the wall, shutting my eyes at the sudden spasm of pain in my skull. On the floor beside me lay a piece of rusty iron pipe wrapped in greasy newsprint that smelled unhappily of fried cod. There was a spray of blood on the newsprint—my blood, I realized. I scrabbled weakly in my coat pocket and discovered that my watch was missing, and of course my purse with it. To put it simply, I'd been bludgeoned and robbed. By now my assailant had no doubt gone to ground in Ashdown forest through one of the common gates.

If I could have felt anything past the pain in my head, I would have felt like a fool, a richly deserving fool. It was no secret that railway thieves booked passage on the South Eastern Railway for no other purpose than to way-lay nighttime travelers at carefully chosen spots along the track. East Sussex is full of forests and empty heath, you see. There's no point in stopping the train to give chase, or to report the incident at the next station, because there's damn-all that anyone can do to put things right. In that part of the country, railway thievery is perhaps the safest line of work there is, unless you're unfortunate enough to run into Tubby Frobisher and be laid out by a blackthorn stick.

Tubby helped me back to my seat, where my companions voiced a general concern. St. Ives probed the back of my head and announced that my skull wasn't crushed. I'd been dealt a sort of sideways blow, to my great good fortune, he said, due to my falling away from the man even as he struck me. To my mind my fortune would have been considerably improved at that moment had I been spared the entire experience.

"What's this now?" St. Ives asked, looking at the newsprint-wrapped pipe, which Tubby had brought away with him.

"The weapon," I muttered stupidly, but then I saw that he didn't mean the length of pipe, but rather the newspaper. He held it up gingerly and unfolded it—the *Brighton Evening Argus*, it turned out to be, from two days past. It was the story on the front page that interested him, and he read it in silence for a time and then laid the newspaper down and looked away. "Of course," he muttered and shook his head tiredly.

Hasbro picked the *Argus* up again and said, "Might I, sir?" St. Ives nodded but said nothing. The salient bits of the remarkable story went thus: A merchant ship, the *India Princess*, out of Brighton, had driven up into the shallows below Newhaven and had stuck fast near where the River Ouse empties into the Channel. She was hauled free when the tide had risen the following morning, with tolerably little damage done to the hull or cargo. Virtually the entire crew had drowned or disappeared, and that was the puzzler. The ship wasn't wrecked. There had been no storm, no foul weather. As remarkable as it might be, they had apparently leapt or fallen over the side shortly after the ship had rounded Selsey Bill, several miles from shore, the lot of them shouting and carrying on like candidates for head nutter at Colney Hatch.

The ship's boy, the sole known survivor of the tragedy, had been asleep, and had awakened when he heard the ruckus. He reported that a fit was even then upon him. He found himself laughing hysterically at nothing and then reeling in sudden terror when his old uncle, dead three years earlier, dressed now in knickers and wearing a fright wig, descended the companionway, grinning fearsomely. In his terror the boy had rushed straight through the apparition and up the companionway to the deck, only to see the first mate and the captain, wrapped in apparently bloody pieces of sail canvas, dancing a hornpipe on the railing. The cook was beating time on an overturned tub, wearing a swab on his head, his face garish with rouge. Other members of the crew staggered about the deck singing and groaning, tearing their hair, jigging in place to the strains of a phantom fiddler. As the boy watched, the two dancing men lost their balance and pitched straight overboard into the sea. The cook, his eyes whirling, picked up the kettle and advanced upon the boy coquettishly, mouthing insanities and beating his head with an enormous galley spoon. His nankeen trousers and shirt were stained with bloody red streaks. The boy trod backward in fear, stepped into the open hatch, and plunged to the lower deck, where he was knocked insensible.

When he came to consciousness he found that the entire crew had disappeared, although the boats were still aboard. His own fit had passed away, and the ghost of his uncle with it. The deck was scattered with trash and overturned kegs. The cook's tub and most of the kitchen tools were thrown about, a cleaver imbedded in the mast. Someone had painted a grinning moon-face on the mainsail, making a general mess of the deck with red paint so that it appeared as if a bloody battle had taken place. Finding that the ship was adrift, the sails flapping, the boy did his best to take her into Brighton, but was at the mercy of the winds, and couldn't manage it alone. The fates favored him, however, because the ship ran on up the Channel, going aground on sandy bottom without disaster. He made his way into Newhaven where he reported the incident, and was immediately taken up on suspicion of having engineered the thing himself. The following morning the drowned bodies of the captain and the cook washed ashore near Littlehampton, their costumes confirming the boy's strange tale. It was a mystery comparable to the recent case of the *Mary Celeste*, and the maritime authorities were at a loss to explain it.

"Well now," Tubby said when Hasbro had finished reading the piece. "Here's another outbreak of lunacy— the third. To my way of thinking the third of anything smacks of a plot, unless this *contagion*, as they call it, is carried on the wind and weather."

"Yes indeed," St. Ives muttered ambiguously, and then he disappeared down into himself again and fell silent, apparently deep in troubled thought. "A plot," he said a moment later. "Poor Alice." Then he said, "A word with you, Hasbro," and the two of them huddled together and spoke in low voices, Hasbro nodding in solemn acquiescence to whatever St. Ives was telling him. I could make out little of what the Professor said beyond his asking Hasbro whether he recalled the death not long past of Lord Busby, Earl of Hampstead, or the Earl of Hamsters, as the press laughingly referred to him. The rest of the talk was mere muttering. It seemed a little thick to me that I was left out of the conversation, although Tubby didn't apparently mind, because he was asleep.

The train soon arrived in Eridge, and we abandoned her for the Cuckoo line to Uckfield, all of us but Hasbro, that is. He mysteriously boarded a London-bound train without so much as a by-your-leave the moment that we climbed down onto the platform. The four of us were now three.

"Hasbro is returning to Chingford to fetch along something that I hope we won't require," St. Ives said. I waited for the explanatory sentence that would surely follow, but it didn't come. It would in the fullness of time, of course, but it was damned strange being left out of things. I was leery of playing the Grand Inquisitor, though, and anyway was too tired to speak. We had been traveling for days it seemed, with only that brief respite at the Half Toad, and the hours had heaped up into a heavy weariness. Tubby was snoring again directly we got underway, and despite the pain in my head I sank toward sleep myself, caught up in a recollection of the shocking condition of Lord Busby's two-days-old corpse when we'd found it.

Busby had been engaged in experiments involving the production of various rays, both visible and invisible, created by the use of large, precious stones. The stones, to the value at tens of thousands of pounds, had been stolen along with his papers and apparatus at the time of his murder. Scotland Yard suspected that he was in league with certain Prussian interests, who were financing his experiments, and St. Ives was of a like mind. The Prussians, perhaps, had simply taken what they wanted when Busby's work had born fruit, and for his efforts had paid poor Busby in lead, as they say.

I tell you this now because my mind is fresh, and because it has a bearing on our story, but there in the train car, at the edge of sleep, I didn't care a brass farthing about Busby one way or the other, given that the man was a traitor, or had been setting up to become one. Take a long spoon when you sup with the devil, I say. In short, I faded from consciousness and slept the sleep of the dead until the train stopped in Uckfield well past midnight.

ABOUT OUR TEDIOUS trek into Blackboys I'll say little. There was no transport to be had in Uckfield, and so, the weather being moderately clear and the night starry, we optimistically set out along the road, hauling our bags in a borrowed handcart. An hour into our journey the sky clouded over and it began to rain in earnest, and despite our umbrellas we were soon soaked through, the mud up to our withers. I was in a bad way by then, leaning heavily against Tubby on the lee side.

News of the peculiar shipwreck had by now changed the general view of things, putting an edge on it, as the knacker would say of his knife. Something was afoot that apparently had little to do with a mere prank involving poisoned punch at the Explorers Club. Tubby, game as ever, was enlivened by the nearness of our goal, and was edgy with the desire push on into Heathfield immediately instead of bothering with Blackboys, and the Tipper be damned. Probably the man was off robbing houses at the moment anyway. It was common sense, Tubby said, that the raid had best be carried out in the early morning hours, when vigilance slept and darkness was an ally.

But I wasn't up to the task. Tubby's idea was that I could bivouac well enough in one of the huts near the coal pits, while he and St. Ives slipped into Heathfield and made their way to the niece's cottage, situated, as it was, on a country lane. The relative isolation of the place would tip the whole business in our favor. They would fling Alice into the back of a hay wagon, and the niece in with her, and spirit both of them out of the village, by stealth, bribery, or main force. They would gather me up and run south, going to ground at Tubby's uncle's place in Dicker.

I was a wreck by then, and far too weary to object. A dark hut near the coal pits would be a welcome thing even if it were crawling with adders, so long as it was dry. I half thought that St. Ives would agree with Tubby, time being of the essence, but about that I was wrong. Instead of seizing the moment as Tubby advised, he reminded us of the asbestos caps, and it was those hats that carried the day, since there was no going into Heathfield without them. He honored us for our loyalty, he said, but it was the Tipper or nothing.

And so it was an hour before dawn when we fell in through the door at the Old Coach Inn on the High Street and roused the innkeeper, still in his nightcap, and moderately unhappy that he'd been deprived of his last hour of sleep. It was wonderful, though, to see what money can do to improve a man's spirit, for he took ours happily enough in the end, and, being short of accommodations, stowed us in two closed up, empty rooms with pieces of dirty carpet on the floor to serve as beds. We'd slept rougher, though, in our time, and the rooms were at least dry. The Professor took one of them, and Tubby and I the other, ours having the added luxury of a solid shutter across the window to block out the day.

Once again I fell into the arms of Morpheus without so much as a heigh-ho. It was several hours later that Tubby arose to heed the call of nature, stumbling over me in the darkness and nearly crushing my hand. I cried out, as you can imagine, and that was the end of sleep. A morbid sun shone through the chinks in the shutter. We rapped on the door of the adjacent room, but apparently the Professor was already up and about. Tubby and I put ourselves together and hastened out into the inn parlor to find our friend, who had solicitously let us sleep—odd behavior under the circumstances, it seemed to me now. The clock began to toll the hour: nine o'clock.

St. Ives was nowhere to be seen, and in fact the inn parlor was generally empty of people. Somehow the journey down the hall from our room had reminded my head of that iron pipe. There was the smell of rashers and coffee leaking out of the kitchen, which on any other morning would suggest the smell of heaven itself, but which gave my stomach an unhappy lurch. I sat down heavily in a chair by the hearth. "I'm all right," I said to Tubby. "It'll pass."

"Of course it will," Tubby said, a little too cheerfully. "That piece of pipe would have knocked the sense out of any other man alive, but you haven't any sense to begin with, Jack, and that's what saved you." He bobbed up and down with silent laughter and then headed· toward the door, meaning to look for our companion. But the door swung open in that very moment, nearly banging into him. A boy of about ten crept in—the stable boy, as it turned out—and stood looking from one to the other of us, twisting an envelope in his hands as if he were wringing out a towel. He was a long-faced lad with a shock of hair that stood up on his head as if he had taken a fright. He touched it to his forehead by way of a greeting.

"Begging your honors' pardon," he said, "but is one of you Mr. Owlesby? Mr. Jack Owlesby?"

"One of us is," I told him. "In fact, I am the very man. Who might you be?"

"John Gunther," he said. And without another word he handed over the envelope, which bore my name across the seal: Jack Owlesby, Esq. I could see at once who had written it. St. Ives's curious back-slanted script is unique. "The man told me to give it to you personal, sir," John Gunther said, "when it was nine by the clock, and to show it to no one else. And I was to give you these." From his pocket he took three guineas and handed them to me. "And now I've done my job and done it fairly, sir."

"So you have, John," I told him, and he stood there goggling at me until I said to Tubby, "Be a good fellow and give Mr. Gunther a token of our esteem, will you Mr. Frobisher? My purse was stolen by blackguards last night, as you might recall."

"Of course," Tubby said. "You can consider it a loan, Jack." He handed over a coin and the boy turned happily toward the door, nearly stumbling into the innkeeper coming in, who cuffed him on the back of the head, cursed him for a slow-belly, and reminded him of his duty. My brain must have been creeping along in sluggish way, for it was only then that the certainty struck me: St. Ives had gone on without us into Heathfield. I bearded the innkeeper before he could take his leave.

Chapter 4

A Day at the Inn

S T. IVES APPARENTLY HADN'T slept at
all, but had sneaked out at dawn and roused the
innkeeper again. He had asked about the Tipper,
and although the innkeeper had warned him against the
man, St. Ives set out down the road in the direction of
the Tipper's shack with a sleepy John Gunther to show
him the way.

"That must have been three hours ago," I said
incredulously.

"Nearly to the minute," the innkeeper said, and then
he went on to tell us that John Gunther had returned
shortly with the missive, but with instructions not to
rouse us, but to wait until we'd come up for air. And so
it was done. The innkeeper had seen to it. He went out

again, promising breakfast and coffee, which sounded distinctly more palatable to me now than it had only a few minutes earlier.

"He's left us in port," Tubby said, slumping into a chair. "And by design. He could as easily have sent the boy back at once to rouse us. For God's sake, man, read the letter, and we'll know why."

I tore it open straightaway, although there was no hurry, as it turned out. "Tubby and Jack," the letter read. "I'm going on into Heathfield without you. I ask your pardon for my deceit, but I can tell you that there is nothing else to be done. I've made a ruin of things in every possible way, and it's my business to sort things out if I can. With the idea of departing at first light, I paid a visit to the Tipper, where he lives below the miners' houses at the bottom of the High Street. The man was unhappy to see me, but he was game enough when he had three of my guineas in his pocket and more promised. He resolutely refused to lead anyone but me into Heathfield. The entire company is out of the question, he maintains, with the roads and paths guarded as they are. He has been in and out twice in the past two days, and it was a close business—work for a cat, he said, and not an elephant.

"Of course I didn't tell him what I was about, and he affected not to care, so long as he received six guineas in all. When we reach our goal, I'll release him from his obligation. He's agreed to return to the inn, find the two of you, make his report, and receive the second payment, which I've entrusted to John Gunther, the stable boy, who is a good lad. By that time, God willing, I'll have thwarted Narbondo's plans and Alice and I will be making our way south to Dicker to look up Tubby's uncle."

I heard Tubby gasp at the mention of Dr. Narbondo's name, but I read on without pause and with precious little surprise:

"When you've paid the Tipper his due, you'd do me a service by leaving straightaway for Dicker yourselves, for we've got further business to attend to in the south. If we're not there by sunset this evening, then I'll leave the two of you to your own devices.

"Many things have become clear to me, Jack, and it's high time that you and Tubby know all. It was Ignacio Narbondo himself who sent the false missive from Dundee, luring us north. I did him the foolish service of dawdling for two weeks, scrutinizing the nonsense that he himself had planted for the very purpose of manipulating me. And it was Narbondo who murdered Busby and stole the gems and his apparatus, suspicion naturally falling to the Prussians. To put it simply, I fear that Narbondo has made use of Busby's Second Ray— a madness ray. I cannot explain the effect of the ray, but I suspect that the gravitational distortion of the energy's waveform provokes a complimentary distortion in the activity of the brain. You'll recall that Busby's portable laboratory was often set up on a prominence. The old Belle Tout Lighthouse at Beachy Head might answer. If it does not, then the device might well be set up within the cliff itself, perhaps in a cavern, where the chalk walls would facilitate the acceleration of the ray, which I fear is impervious to the horizon. That would explain the curious matter of the Explorers Club. Narbondo's submarine vessel has been sighted often enough near Eastbourne...."

"Narbondo!" Tubby said, unable to contain his loathing any longer. "I'll give that bloody reptile a taste of my blackthorn stick this time. See if I don't!"

"Pray that we have the opportunity," I said, waving him silent.

"You recall the experiment with Busby's sapphire propulsion lamp," the letter went on, "the way the crystal structure of the sapphire was destroyed in a single use. This is much the same, except that the lamp that transmits the madness ray makes use of an emerald. Even Narbondo's coffers cannot support the continual destruction of emeralds, and I suspect that the three trials have cost him dearly. Busby had discovered a way to dissolve the emerald in acid, and then reconstruct it under high heat, so that the crystalline lattice would be perfect, impervious to the degenerative effects of the device. In short, Narbondo will want this fortified emerald, which Busby gave to me for safekeeping, although I fear that there is no such thing as safekeeping.

"Busby was in great fear for his life there in Scarborough. I was to return the emerald to him in a fortnight if his fears were unfounded. Alas, they were not. Clearly it took Narbondo some time to discover that an unfortified emerald would deteriorate, but Busby's notes *must* have mentioned the existence of the fortified emerald, and, I suspect, mentioned my name along with it. If not, then Narbondo would have no need to involve me at all. To the contrary, he would have a free hand with things, and the Crown, perhaps the planet, would be at his mercy. Hence my sending Hasbro to Chingford to retrieve the fortified emerald, which is the most valuable card in our hand. But in the end it must be destroyed, even if it means my own destruction. Narbondo can be tempted by it. It will draw him out. *But he must not be allowed to possess it.* If I'm taken, the ransom demand will shortly follow. I've tarried long enough. *Sharp's the word!*"

This last was heavily underscored, with a blot of ink at the end where the tip of the nib had snapped off. The four of us who had set out from Victoria Station just a few hours ago were now two.

"Feedle-de-de," Tubby said, immensely unhappy. "Clearly he shouldn't have gone into Heathfield alone, not with this much at stake. *Elephants!*"

"Surely that wasn't directed at you," I told him. "It was meant to be a what? A metaphor, not an insult."

"I know that, you oaf. What I mean to say is that the venture *wanted* an elephant. He should have seen that. It was damned reckless of him not to. What's this business of the lure and the prey?"

"For my money," I told him, "it means that Narbondo fabricated a letter from Thomas Bouch to draw St. Ives north to Scotland. Then, discovering that Alice had fortuitously gone on to Heathfield, he orchestrated this uncanny outbreak of madness, understanding full well that St. Ives would race straight into the heart of danger upon his return."

"*Orchestrated it*? So this entire thing was a ploy? What about the business at the Explorers Club, and the ship run aground? What does that have to do with St. Ives?"

"Nothing and everything," I told him. "I'd guess that they were merely trials. Narbondo effected them from out on Beachy Head. Do you know that our watch salesman bought a ticket last night on the *Beachy Head Runner*? I did a bit of sleuthing there at Victoria Station, after you'd gone home after your things."

"Is that right?" Tubby said. "The blithering pie-faced devil. I should have beaten the man where he stood. But of course you're neglecting the fact that scores of people bought that same ticket. We did, for instance, at least as far as Eridge."

"As did the railway thief." I said, everything coming clear to me now. "It fits, don't you see? Narbondo wouldn't want an army of us in Heathfield. Given another couple of minutes and your railway thief would have tumbled me from the car, hidden himself once again, and knocked you on the head as well, or Hasbro, when one of you came along. Robbery was convenient, but perhaps it wasn't the motive."

"And that's why the blighter was setting in to finish you off when I dealt him that blow," Tubby said. "He'd already taken your purse, after all. There was no point in murdering you for mere sport."

"No point at all," I said.

"One might say that he was attempting to hack the legs off the elephant before it lumbered into Heathfield."

"There's perhaps more truth than poetry in your phrasing, but it's as you say. There's a good chance I owe you my life."

"As well as the half crown I gave the boy just now."

"That was no half crown," I said, calling his shameless bluff. "I clearly saw you give the boy a shilling."

"God's rabbit!" Tubby said. "I'll need that break-fast directly. My big guts are eating my little guts, and without salt." As if his command were a wish on a genie's lamp, breakfast arrived, interrupting our parlay.

Maddeningly, there was nothing for it but to wait. St. Ives had declared it necessary. The absence of asbestos caps declared it necessary. The two of us would sit on our hands in Blackboys and be satisfied with our lot, hoping to God that the Tipper would appear, and quickly, although to my mind it was a long shot. Like as not the Tipper was just another rum mug in the employ of Ignacio Narbondo—another person for St. Ives to knock on the head if he were to prevail in Heathfield.

We idled away the balance of the morning browsing through the books in the inn parlor. I made inroads into Southey's *Life of Nelson*. Tubby dipped into Andrew Marvel's *Bachelor*, perpetually interrupting himself to look out of the windows with an expectant squint in his eye. Now and then he stood up, grasped his stick, and flailed away at an enemy that only he could perceive. Hours later, after endless rounds of two-handed Whist and flagons of tea, we ate a roasted duck stuffed with potatoes while watching ever more intently for the door to open and the Tipper to walk in and announce himself. But although the door did just that off and on, and any number of people walked in or walked out, there was no sign of the Tipper. We whiled away the last hour of daylight at a table near the fire over a beaker of port, the rain still falling, half a dozen people sitting around the parlor taking their ease.

The inn door slammed opened, and, as you can imagine, we both looked up sharply. Once again, it wasn't the Tipper. It was Alice, looking like a wildly beautiful Ophelia, her dark hair windblown, her dress and coat splashed with mud, a haunted look in her eyes. In her hand she clutched what could only be one of the asbestos caps. She gaped at the two of us, cried out, "Oh, Jack!" and fell to the floor in a dead faint.

Chapter 5

Treachery in
Heathfield

THAT SAME MORNING, WHILE the
sun was still low on the horizon and Tubby and
I slept, St. Ives followed the Tipper into the
woods. It was nearly dark beneath the oak trees and the
Scots pine. Steam rose from the wet leaves and needles
that covered the forest floor, creating a ground fog. St.
Ives carried an asbestos hat, but the Tipper told him
that until they were on the very outskirts of Heathfield
itself, the cap was of no value to him. In Heathfield it
would be priceless. He declined to respond to the questions St. Ives put to him. He had been paid his fee to
take St. Ives into Heathfield, he said, not to palaver like
a jackdaw.

Soon the ground itself grew black with coal dust, and the forest opened onto a heath as blighted as the Cities of the Plain after the hail of brimstone. There were mountains of coal dug out of the pits, which descended some 150 fathoms into the depths of the earth—deep enough, the Tipper pointed out, to bury a mort of corpses. Rusting coal tubs lay roundabout, and ruined iron machinery, and heaps of firebrick, fabricated by the hundreds of tons to be shipped off to smelters, and all of it covered with black dust where the dust wasn't washed off by the elements.

The coal pits were quiet, it being the morning of the Sabbath, but there was a low hovel with smoke coming out of a chimney, with a stream that flowed alongside it, the water running black. The Tipper led St. Ives on a circuitous route, behind the pallets of firebrick and outbuildings, wary of the watchman in the hovel. They crossed the stream on a footbridge, the morning growing darker rather than lighter, and before long a spewy sort of rain started in. The Tipper vowed that if he had known that the weather would turn on them, he'd have asked for something more than six guineas for his trouble. Out of fairness, he said, the Professor should pay him the rest of his fee at once, and not compel him to wait for it, since the result was the same in either case, and if they were discovered and pursued, it was every man for himself. If he were captured, he would be three guineas to the bad.

"Aye," said St. Ives. "But a man with something to look forward to is likely to do his work more cheerfully, and not retire early from the field. And in the situation you describe, I'd be the one who's three guineas to the bad, wouldn't I?"

The Tipper lapsed again into silence, and they went on, into the forest once more, leaving the coal dust behind them. Near Heathfield, the fog rose again around their knees, with here and there patches of it ascending into the treetops. "Pray this fog ain't washed out by the rain," the Tipper said. "A fog is perfect weather for a lark like this."

His prayer was answered, for the fog grew heavier as the minutes slipped away and they neared the point where they'd don the caps. The Tipper slowed, held out a restraining hand, and whispered, "Steady-on!" And then, when all was still, "Listen!"

There was a distant mutter of voices, not the lunatic voices of a village gone mad, but of reasonable men, several of them. How close they were, it was impossible to say. The fog hid the world from view and obscured sound. The Tipper turned to St. Ives and in a low voice said, "So much as a quack from your lordship, and I'm gone, do you hear me? You'll not see me again. I'll go back after the payment that's waiting for me in Blackboys and tell your friends that everything's topping. You'll be on your own."

"Agreed," St. Ives said, and the Tipper muttered something about it's not making a halfpenny's difference who agreed with what. They moved forward carefully, keeping hidden, until they could see a road ahead, the fog blowing aside to reveal a small company of red-coated soldiers sitting beneath an open canvas tent.

"Lobsters," the Tipper whispered. "Up from Brighton, no doubt." He nodded toward a dense birch copse some distance farther on, which ran right up against the road. "That's where we cross into Heathfield proper. Put that cap on. Pull it low over your ears. If you lose the cap, you'll lose your wits with it, although you won't know you've lost either of them, if you ken my meaning."

St. Ives donned the cap, which was indeed cobbled together from a pair of gloves, the fingers rising atop like the comb of a rooster. He tugged it firmly down over his ears, deadening what little sound was left in the quiet morning. He had no real understanding of the science involved in the caps, although he suspected that the answer lay somewhere within the notebooks of Lord Busby. More to the point, he wondered how the Tipper could have discovered the efficacy of the asbestos cloth. He couldn't have, of course. Even if the gloves were ready to hand, it wouldn't have come into his mind to sew them into a cap. The Tipper was clearly in the hire of someone who had knowledge of such things. Busby being dead, that someone's identity was obvious.

When would the betrayal come? St. Ives wondered, watching the Tipper scuttle on ahead toward the stand of birch. Soon, surely. He felt for the bulge of the pistol tucked inside his waistcoat. Then he reached into his vest pocket and drew out a hastily written letter addressed to Alice. He hadn't had time to write what he meant— couldn't find the words to say it. But if it were necessary, and if the fates were willing, he could get the pitiful attempt into Alice's hands even if he were captured, and she might at least win free and remember him for who he had always meant to be, paving his marriage with good intentions.

He crumpled the letter into his vest again, where it would be within easy reach, and then hastened forward to where the Tipper stood a few steps back from the edge of the road. The two of them might be hazily visible through the fog when they crossed, although for the moment they were hidden from view. The Tipper mouthed something incomprehensible, but made his meaning clear with a gesture. They crept out into the open, looking carefully north, and for a moment they caught sight of the soldiers again, mere shadows in the murk, before slipping into the forest on the Heathfield side of the road.

St. Ives experimentally tugged his cap away from his ear, and instantly, as if the space within his mind had been occupied by a ready-built dream, he had the strange notion that he was at a masquerade ball. He had never been a dancer, and he loathed costumes, but now he was elated at the idea of taking a turn about the floor. He saw Alice approaching, although she was a mere wraith, which didn't strike him as at all odd. She carried a glass of punch, seeming to float toward him atop a shifting bed of leaves. He could see forest shrubbery through her, and an uncanny white mist roiling behind her like smoke. Something was happening to her face. It was melting, like a wax bust in a fire.

He yanked the cap back down, pressing his hands tightly against his ears. Now there was no Alice, no masquerade. The madness had slipped in like an airborne poison as soon as the door had swung open, and then had evaporated when the door had slammed shut. And yet despite the cap there seemed to be some presence lurking at the edge of his mind, some creature just kept at bay, but straining to be loosed from its bonds. As they neared the village the capering presence in his head became more insistent. He began to hear small, murmuring voices that rose and fell like a freshening wind. Quite distinctly he heard the voice of his mother saying something about a piano. He imagined himself sitting happily on the parlor floor of his childhood home, dressed in knee breeches, watching a top careen around in a wobbly spin, its buzzing sound clear in his ears.

It came into his mind that his cap might be inferior, that it might be compromised somehow. The Tipper seemed to be sober enough. St. Ives compelled himself to put up a mental struggle, recalling algebraic theorems, settling on Euclid's lemma, picturing prime numbers falling away like dominoes. He added them together as they ran, tallying sums. A bell began to ring, in among the numbers, it seemed to him, but then ceased abruptly, replaced by the sound of a fiddler, the fiddling turning to laughter, the numbers in his mind blowing apart like dandelion fluff. He forced himself to think of Alice, of himself having gone away to Scotland on his fruitless mission while she journeyed south, possibly to her doom.

The branch of a shrub along the path lashed at his face, sobering him further. He saw a cottage ahead through the thinning trees now, recognizing the blue shutters. On beyond the cottage lay the broad heath from whence the village got its name. The Tipper had taken St. Ives straight to the cottage, despite its remote location: clearly he knew the way well enough. He stood just ahead now, his finger to his lips.

The fog had deepened, and not an imaginary fog. St. Ives could smell it, the damp of it on the stones of the cottage, the musty leaves. It recalled the holidays of his youth, spent in Lyme Regis. Memories of seaside vistas wavered pictorially now on the fog itself, like images in a magic lantern show. He reached out to take hold of them, thinking that he might literally hold them, and he was saddened when they passed through his fingers as mere mist.

The Tipper was grinning at him, as if enjoying St. Ives's mental unmooring. He put his fingers to his lips and whistled, and out of the fog came Alice herself, not at all a wraith, but solid now, walking slowly as if mesmerized. Her eyes were distant, gazing out on heaven-knew-what. The sight of her brought St. Ives instantly to himself. A man walked behind her, holding onto a clutch of fabric at the back of her dress and wearing one of the asbestos caps.

Then she quite apparently saw St. Ives, for she shook her head as if to dislodge the cobwebs and focused on his face in apparent amazement. This partial return to the waking world seemed to stagger her, and she stumbled forward, nearly falling. The man behind her hauled her to her feet again. St. Ives saw then that he was none other than Sam Burke, the Peddler, dressed in his familiar tweeds.

The Tipper suddenly loomed in front of St. Ives and, quick as a snake, his empty hand disappeared inside St. Ives's waistcoat and reappeared with the pistol in it. He stepped back, shrugging. "This'll do just as well as the three guineas," he said. From behind the corner of the house a third man stepped into view, his right arm tied into a sling. In his left hand he held a pistol of his own, which he pointed at Alice, no doubt as a message to St. Ives, since Alice seemed to have gone out of her mind again and was indifferent to it.

A wave of anger washed the confusion from the Professor's brain, and he threw himself forward, hitting the surprised Tipper a heavy backhand blow that knocked him down. The pistol flew from his hand, but St. Ives ignored it. Without pause he snatched the Tipper's cap from the man's head and shoved it into his own waistband. He clutched the Tipper's neck with his right hand and lifted him bodily off the ground so that he hung by his own weight, his feet kicking, his mouth opening and closing like the mouth of a fish drawn from deep water. The one-armed man still pointed his pistol at Alice. He stepped forward now, shaking his head at St. Ives, and in that moment St. Ives knew that the man wouldn't shoot either of them. The pistol was a bluff.

St. Ives made a sudden lunge forward, carrying the Tipper with him, clutched to his chest, the Tipper biting and lurching insanely, a low, gibbering nose uttering from his mouth. Pivoting on his right foot and spinning halfway around, St. Ives hurled the Tipper like a sack of potatoes at the man with the pistol, both of them going over in a heap. He reached into his vest and drew out the note that he had written earlier that morning, and then, rushing toward the Peddler and Alice, he yanked the Tipper's hat from his waistband, shoved the note into it, and with both hands pulled the cap down over Alice's head and ears, turning sideways in that same moment and bowling into the Peddler, knocking him backward and clubbing at his head with his fists.

The Peddler grappled him, strong as an ape, reeling back against the wall of the cottage. He heard Alice shout something—no sort of madness, but something sensible—and he shouted back at her, "Run! Run!" at the top of his voice, holding on to the Peddler, pressing his thumb into the man's throat, compressing his larynx. And then his own cap was snatched off his head, and there was a shout of triumph in his ear. Abruptly he heard fiddling and laughter on the wind, a cacophony of wild noise. There was a gunshot, fearfully close, and he saw Alice running, the one armed man pointing the pistol and firing it over her head and into the trees. St. Ives looked back vaguely at the man he was throttling, confused now, and saw with horror that the man wore the contorted face of his own father.

St. Ives reeled backward, releasing the man's neck. Smoke seemed to him to be pouring out of the windows of the cottage now, taking the form of grinning demons as it roiled into the air. The world was a reeling inferno in the moment before he was struck in the back of the head and darkness descended upon him.

Chapter 6

Alice's Story

MOMENTS AFTER HER COLLAPSE on the floor of the inn parlor, Alice revived, and of course we helped her to her feet and into a chair. For a time she sat there with her eyes closed, catching her breath and her sensibilities, still clutching the cap. When she opened her eyes again they had a steadier sort of look in them, as if she had returned in spirit as well as body and mind. From inside the cap she drew out a crushed piece of paper, then threw the cap angrily into the corner of the room.

Tubby made straightaway to our table to fetch a flagon of tea and a cup. She drank the tea down gratefully, and then after another moment's rest, happily took a glass of port. She thanked the both of us, looking somewhat recovered, but in no wise happy.

"We've been waiting all day for word of St. Ives," I said to her anxiously.

"I've got all the word there is," she told us, "and none of it good."

—◦◦◦—

THE MADNESS THAT had possessed her for the past three days had diminished when St. Ives put the asbestos cap upon her head, and had evaporated utterly when she was well clear of Heathfield. Of the madness itself, she recalled that some of it was wonderful, some of it horrifying, but the memory of it was already fading from her mind, as if it had been a waking dream, even now only a memory of a memory.

Some few days previously she and the niece Sydnee had been strolling through the village, where the spring Cuckoo Fair was just then getting underway. The streets were awash with people, with dozens in the costume of St. Richard and with feast booths set up and a great deal of merriment that the weather couldn't dampen. The legendary cuckoo was on display, looking something like a large pigeon that someone had waxed artistic with. The two of them had stopped to hobnob with the bird, when suddenly, without warning of any sort, although Alice faintly recalls a high-pitched keening in the air, the world, in her words, "tipped sideways." On the instant the feast day merriment turned to mayhem. She found herself sitting in the road, with the odd certainty that she was the literal embodiment of the Heathfield cuckoo. She remembered chuckling out loud there in the street—not laughing, mind you, but chuckling like a hen on a nest—convinced that her dress was woven of feathers rather than merino wool.

She recalls Sydnee wandering off, snatching at the air as if trying to catch a will-o'-the-wisp, and in the days that followed Alice never once saw her niece again, or didn't know her if she did. Those days might as well have been moments or years, her sense of the passing of time having abdicated. She somehow found her way home to the cottage, where she conversed with hobgoblins and wraiths, although the hobgoblins might simply have been the Tipper and his cronies.

She fell silent for a time after telling us this, and then in a smaller voice said, "I left him there. I simply fled. It was what he wished—what he commanded. And yet it was cowardice on my part. There was a fallen pistol that I might have reached, had I acted instead of standing there stupefied. There was also that horrible man aiming his own pistol at me. He was injured, though. His arm was in a sling. I might have prevailed over him." She stared into the purple depths of the port. "I fled through the woods, right into the midst of the soldiers at the blockade. I had removed the cap by then, and at first they assumed I was insane, and perhaps I still was, a bit. I told them that a man had been assaulted, because I didn't know what else to call it, but they were in no haste to venture into Heathfield. I bid them good day and quite coolly walked away into the woods and came here, every step of the way thinking I should turn back, regretting that I had left St. Ives in such peril."

"By God they would have shot you, too, Alice, if you had," Tubby told her sensibly. "You must see that. Your value to them was to draw St. Ives into Heathfield. Once you had, you were worth nothing. Jack and I would have been sitting here playing Whist while the two of you disappeared out of existence. But here you are, alive and well, *precisely* because you weren't rash. Now we three can put our considerable shoulders to the wheel."

"You're wrong," she said. "They allowed me to go. They want something, and they believe that I might provide it for them. They wouldn't have hindered me."

"Perhaps," Tubby said. "But in any event you were better out of it. And they wouldn't have *had* to kill you. They'd simply have had to remove your cap. You couldn't have prevailed against them. The three of us might, however."

I half listened to Tubby's assurances, but I had been shocked to stony silence by Alice's pronouncements. St.

Ives taken? It was almost too much for me to grasp, even though I had feared that very thing. There were indeed three of us, but clearly there was only the one cap, and no time to find the elusive "wheel" that we were to put our shoulders to. I couldn't abide waiting. I strode to the corner full of bloody-minded thoughts and plucked up the cap, looking out the window toward the edge of the forest, which was dark now. There was no question of the identity of the man with his arm in a sling, nor any question of his being a cold-blooded devil. Alice had described the third man: clearly the Peddler, but at that moment I didn't much care if he was Beelzebub in a dogcart.

Tubby saw what I was up to with the cap straightaway. "Don't be unwise, Jack," he said, taking me by the arm. "Alice has just escaped from that mire of human scum. There's no sense in your wading back in."

"There's but the one cap," I told him, as if that justified my going alone or at all.

"And there's no telling how many of the villains are at work. St. Ives sees things far more clearly than either of us. Now that the prey has fallen into the trap, they'll almost certainly return to Beachy Head. The battle of Heathfield was lost, although thank God Alice was not. Your visiting the scene of the battle can't come to anything useful. At best it's a mere delay. We'll do what St. Ives asked and take the battle to them, by heaven. It wasn't but half an hour ago that you were telling me the same thing. Listen to yourself if you won't listen to me, but listen to yourself sober, for God's sake, and not drunk on anger."

There was of course a great deal of sense in what he said, although I still couldn't see more than a red glimmer of it. But then Alice prevailed upon me to read the message on the folded piece of foolscap that she had found in the cap—apparently the first of the two messages that St. Ives had written out that morning, for the nib of the pen was still sharp.

"Dearest Alice…" it began, and what followed was the plea of a man whose hopes were defeated. His first concern, you see, was to put things right between the two of them. But Alice's tears as we silently read the note made it clear that she had no idea that things had gone wrong, no earthly notion of the Professor's misery, the ebbing of his hope, as if he believed that love was as shifting and transitory as the tides. What strange things we convince ourselves of when the shadows descend upon us!

In short, the first part of the note, written hastily in the darkness of the early morning hours, is none of our business here.

"Follow the track east into the sun," the message read. "Across the road and some two miles farther on, you'll find the coal pits, which Tubby Frobisher tells us consumes a considerable acreage. It's his invaluable knowledge of the area that I depend on here. The path that skirts the pits will come out of the forest directly behind the Old Coach Inn, Blackboys, where Tubby and Jack will be waiting. If I'm taken, my guess is that it'll be to Beachy Head. Narbondo's goal is ransom, not murder, although murder might follow the ransom, as it often does. If you're reading this, then I'm no longer the captain of my fate. Adieu, Alice."

That was the long and the short of it, although the "adieu" was preceded by another profession of his love, as if the first wasn't convincing. There was an irony at work here. Alice had been driven mad by the machinations of a human monster, and St. Ives had rushed impetuously into danger to rescue her. Now their roles were reversed, and it was Alice's turn to play the hero, for she wouldn't be talked into returning home to Chingford under any circumstances, despite both Tubby and I bringing the cannons of logic to bear upon her flank, so to speak. Alice had a single contentious desire, and that was to find St. Ives and to bring him out of bondage alive.

The mention of the fortified emerald brought up more questions than it answered, so we left Alice to read the note that John Gunther had brought to us that morning, and set out down the hallway to fetch our bags. In a little over an hour there was a southward-bound mail coach that would take us on into Dicker, and the three of us were determined to be on it. We would spend the night at Tubby's uncle's house, find Alice some suitable accoutrements, and lay out our plan. However it fell out, the three of us would not go quite so impetuously into the environs of Beachy Head as St. Ives had gone into Heathfield.

Chapter 7

Ransom

I T TOOK BUT A moment to ready ourselves for the trip south. The coach sat in the yard, the coach-man eating his supper inside. We had forty minutes of waiting, and were determined not to stand idle. There was no telling what we would find at Beachy Head or along the way, but it might easily be further outbreaks of madness, in which case we wanted for asbestos caps, which meant paying the Tipper's residence a visit. Tubby insisted that with a little luck we might manage to burn his shack to the ground, but Alice wasn't keen on the idea of gambling away the higher stakes by engaging in irrelevant pleasures, nor was she keen on remaining at the inn while Tubby and I went off on the errand. The Tipper wouldn't be there, we assumed. Surely he wouldn't be so brazen as to return to Blackboys, knowing that Alice had escaped and that the two of us waited at the inn.

We went out then, the night blessedly dry and with a shred of moonlight. In the stable we found our young friend helping the coach horses to bags of oats. He leapt up like a jack-in-the-box when he saw us and asked could he be of service. Perhaps Tubby *had* given him a half crown, for he was singularly anxious to oblige us. We asked merely that he describe the Tipper's shack, which he did with particular care.

"It's a low hovel of a place," he said, "that sits alone at the bottom of the road near the forest. There's a pile of old trash you'll see alongside, and the door is half a-hanging. One of the great rusty hinges is broke-like, and the top of the door is fixed with a hook and eye. It's a lazy man's dodge, and a bloke could find his way in easy enough by setting a pry bar into the gap or knocking out that hook."

"I see that you're a sharp one, Mr. Gunther," Tubby said, giving him a wink. "Will you do us another service now?" The boy replied that he would, anything we required, all the time goggling at Alice. "Don't mention at all that we've been round talking to you," Tubby told him. "And if anything out of the way happens at the Tipper's shack tonight, perhaps you'd be good enough to know nothing at all about it or about the three of us either."

"I ain't heard nothing," he said, making a key-turning motion in front of his lips. "I hate the bloody Tipper. Nothing but cuffs and curses from the likes of him, and him a bleeding midget, begging your lady's pardon."

"And don't let the mail coach go on without us," Tubby said, giving him another half crown, which he accepted gleefully, it apparently being his lucky day.

With that we left our bags in his care and went along down the High Street in a singular hurry, but silent as phantoms, past two blocks of miners' cottages, with more set behind them in rows. The village was quiet on the damp Sabbath evening, people staying indoors, which was to the good if Alice had some sort of mischief on her mind. She has as much pluck as does St. Ives, although she is, if I might say it, far easier to look at than the Professor, who is growing tolerably craggy as the years pass. Alice has what might be called a natural beauty, which strikes you even if she's just come in out of a storm or from mucking about in the garden. She's moderately tall, very fit, with eyes that are just a little bit piercing, as if she sees things, you included, particularly clearly. Her dark hair is perhaps her best feature—perpetually a little wild and refusing to stay pinned down, something like the woman herself. I write all this in the interests of literary accuracy, of course. My own betrothed, Dorothy Keeble, a beauty of a different stamp, would tell you the same about Alice, who has become her great good friend.

The Tipper's hovel sat conveniently alone, a good distance below the rest of the village, partway down a grassy decline: our good luck, for we wouldn't be easily heard or seen. It was just as the boy had described it, right down to the junk pile and the badly hung door with its makeshift hinge, which you could see easily enough in the moonlight that shone on the front wall. We were crossing the last patch of ground when we saw a glim of light inside the hovel, right along the edge of a curtain, as if someone had opened the slide on a dark lantern to see what he was about.

"*Here's* a bit of luck," whispered Tubby. "He's sneaked back after his swag, I'll warrant, before clearing out. I'll just see to the front door, and you two go around to the back, eh? He'll have a bolt-hole. No doubt he'll make for the woods."

We set out without a moment to spare across the wet grass, thankful for the curtains on the window, which would hide us as well as they would hide the Tipper, if it was him mucking around inside. Tubby of course carried his blackthorn stick with him, but I had no sort of weapon, and neither did Alice. There in the weedy trash, however, lay a serendipitous length of rusted pipe, which I snatched up in passing. Despite my rough treatment aboard the train, the idea of similarly bashing anyone with a length of pipe didn't much appeal to me, although the idea of the Tipper slipping away from us appealed even less, and I was determined to do the useful thing.

We had scarcely taken up our position outside the rear door when there was the crash of the front door coming down, a shout from Tubby, and the sound of running feet. I raised the length of pipe and was moving forward when the door flew open and the Tipper hurled himself down the several wooden steps, wearing a slouch hat and carrying a canvas bag. He was clearly intent upon making for the safety of the woods, which would have been easy enough if it were only Tubby in pursuit. I stepped in front of him, however, crouching down, drawing back the piece of pipe like a cricket bat. He endeavored to slow himself, but gravity had helped impel him down the steps, and now the hillside was doing the same. He rushed at me headlong, swinging the canvas bag and slamming me on the shoulder with it, knocking me sideways. I swung my piece of pipe as I fell, clipping him neatly on the back of the leg behind the knee. The bag flew out of his hands, sailing away toward Alice as he sprawled forward. Alice picked the bag up, and the thing was done.

Tubby came out then, puffing and blowing like a whale. "Looks like a pawnbroker's shop inside," he said.

Miraculously, despite his tumble, the Tipper still wore his slouch hat, which Tubby plucked from his head now, cuffing him twice across the face with it. "You're in the presence of a lady, you goddamned rascal," he said, and then he sailed the hat away down the hill, where it settled over the top of a moonlit stone. The Tipper looked at us hatefully, a human bomb about to detonate.

Alice tugged open the drawstrings of the bag and peered inside, reaching in and pulling out two of the asbestos caps and tossing them to me. "Sydnee's silver," she said, taking another look. "Tableware and candelabra." She reached inside and drew out a clasp purse, which she snapped open. "Jewelry—Sydnee's jewelry—and a good lot of coin. Here's my broach, too, and my necklace...."

"You *crawling* piece of filth," Tubby said to the Tipper, raising the blackthorn stick menacingly. The Tipper cringed away, certain that he was about to be pummeled, but Alice sensibly shook her head at Tubby.

"Into the house with him," she said, "quickly."

In an unwise moment I latched onto the Tipper's coat, twisting it in my fist and yanking him to his feet. More quickly than I could follow, he snatched a dirk from a scabbard in his boot and took a swipe at my arm, tearing through the sleeve of my coat. I felt the blade slice through skin, a sharp pain, and a wash of warm blood on my forearm. In my surprise I let go of the handful of coat and reeled back, sitting down hard. The Tipper lurched away toward the woods again, running like a hare. Tubby swarmed past me in pursuit, but it was an uneven race, and by the time I had joined in, gripping my bleeding arm, the Tipper had already disappeared into the shadow of the forest.

Tubby returned, looking immensely unhappy. I could do nothing but apologize, although of course there was no point in it. None of us had seen the dirk, after all, and it might have gone even worse for one of us if things had fallen out differently. "I'm all right," I said, when I saw Alice's anxiety. I pressed my coat and shirtsleeve hard against the wound and gave her my best smile.

In we went without another word. The Tipper's lantern was still lit, sitting where it had sat when Tubby pried open the door, which hung out across the threshold now, aslant the bottom hinge. The place was littered with stolen goods—porcelain objects, bric-a-brac, paintings, furs and other garments. The Tipper had been a busy little thief. How he intended to flee with the goods I can't say, unless he had a cart waiting somewhere. Perhaps he had returned merely to take out the coin and the jewelry and meant to leave the rest. We didn't have time to puzzle it out, for we couldn't brook any delay. Our mail coach would soon be standing idle on our account, and we had an aversion to calling attention to ourselves and even more of being left behind.

We dressed the wound on my arm with gin and with a silk scarf as a bandage and went out through the back door again, shutting it after us, Alice carrying the canvas bag. I felt first rate, I can tell you, despite my sliced-up arm. We had put our hands on the swag and had two more caps into the bargain, should we need them. We hadn't ended the Tipper's depredations, but we'd taken some of the wind out of his sails—real progress, it seemed to me, and the whole job hadn't taken a half hour.

The coach waited in the yard, the horses stamping and whinnying, the wind out of the south with the faint smell of salt on it. John Gunther stood with our luggage looking anxious. When he saw us he hurried across, holding out what appeared to be a stiffish envelope. Alice took it from him.

"A man give this to me directly you went down to the Tipper's," the boy said. "He was an ugly article, with a head like the moon."

"Dressed in brown tweed?" I asked him.

"That's the one."

"The Peddler!" I said to Tubby as Alice slipped a largish photograph out of the envelope, tilting it toward the gas lamp to see it clearly. Something came over her face then, and it seemed to me that she went as pale as she had been when she had walked into the inn an hour ago. She steadied herself and handed me the photograph, which reeked of chemicals. It was of Langdon St. Ives, lying in a wooden coffin. At first I thought he was dead, and I simply couldn't breathe, but he was not. He was evidently mad, his eyes opened unnaturally wide, as if he were staring at some descending horror. His forearms were raised, his hands half closed so that they appeared to be claws. At the bottom of the photograph, in a scrawl of grease pen, were the words, "Belle Tout Light. Eleven in the morning. Bring the stone."

The meaning was clear. They hadn't sent the message with Alice when they allowed her to flee from Heathfield, because they intended to underscore the demand with the photograph, which was a hellish obscenity. They had made a tolerably quick business of it—anticipated our movements, too, as we stumbled about imagining ourselves to be acting, when in fact we had inevitably been acted upon.

I tipped the photograph into the flame of the gas lamp until it blazed, burning down to my fingers before I dropped it to the cobbles of the courtyard and ground it beneath my heel. My recently elevated mood had vanished. I regretted letting the Tipper get the better of me. I regretted Tubby's having prevented me from going into Heathfield alone. I regretted not having been at the Inn when the Peddler delivered the photograph. The night was suddenly a hailstorm of regrets. I told myself that I might yet see the whole crowd of villains hanging from gibbets, but it was cold comfort.

Alice very calmly asked John Gunther if he would do us one final service. She even managed to smile at the boy, who was staring at my bloody coat sleeve now, apprehension in his eyes. After our departure, Alice told him, he was to fetch the constable and say that he had been out taking the air when he'd seen someone coming out through the Tipper's door, which was broken from its hinges, and making away downhill. She put another coin into the boy's hand, and he nodded reassuringly. The three of us turned to the coach, as impatient as the coachman to be on our way. Our business in Blackboys was at an end. The authorities would find the leftover swag before anyone else thought to loot the place. When sanity returned to Heathfield, as it perhaps already had, the Tipper's victims might at least recover what they'd lost.

The three of us climbed into the empty coach, which swayed as if on heavy seas as Tubby hoisted himself aboard. The driver hied-up the horses and away we went down the road toward Dicker, rattling and creaking along. The moon was high in the sky now, and the forest trees along the roadside shone with a silver aura, the wind just brisk enough to move the branches.

Chapter 8

On the Side
of the Angels

ST. IVES ABRUPTLY CAME to himself, waking up fully sensible, but with no idea where he had been a moment earlier. Now he lay in the back of a moving wagon that smelled of hay, and in fact he rested comfortably enough on that substance, looking up in the faint light at what was apparently tightly stretched canvas. His hands and feet were bound, although the rope that connected his ankles had some play in it, enough so that he could hobble if he had any place to hobble to. He could recall the scuffle at Heathfield, and Alice's flight, but precious little else since then, aside from a suspicious memory of having met the Queen, who had taken the form of an immense jackdaw wearing a tall golden crown. Other memories flitted through his mind—a trip to Surrey in a cart drawn by a pig, a flight over London on an enormous bullet fired out of a cannon on Guy Fawkes day, a descent into the depths of hell where he held a long conversation with a crestfallen devil who looked very much like himself. He knew that he had been insane and that he was now in the hands of his enemies, but whether for hours or days he couldn't say. Nor could he tell in which direction the wagon traveled, only that they moved at a moderate pace, bumping and jostling along over an ill-maintained road.

After a time the driver reined in the horses, and all was momentarily still. St. Ives closed his eyes, feigning sleep. The gate of the wagon clattered downward, and as the night wind swirled in around him there was the swishing sound of the canvas being drawn back. The wagon dipped on its springs as someone climbed aboard, and then there was the sharp reek of ammonia under his nose, and his eyes flew open involuntarily. A voice said, "That roused the bugger," and immediately he was dragged bodily off the back of the cart and dumped onto the ground, still bound.

For a moment he lay there, wary of being kicked, but the men—the Peddler Sam Burke and the man with his arm in a sling—walked off and left him to his own devices. He sat up, grateful to breathe clean air, and looked up through the trees at the moon riding at anchor amid a flotilla of stars, which told him that they were traveling south. *Beachy Head*, he thought, smelling the sea on the wind now. It was pretty much the same moon that had risen last night—only a few bare hours having passed since he had been taken. They weren't on the Dicker road by any means, but were on a broad sort of path through the forest, little wider than the wagon.

In a small clearing nearby, his companions had set up a low table, with a Soyer's Magic Stove alongside it, the wick already lit. The Peddler was just then filling a kettle with water, which he set on the stove, and then from a basket he took out candles, a teapot and cups, a loaf of bread and a piece of what looked like farmhouse cheddar, all of which he set out on the table, arranging it neatly, as if he took particular pleasure in what he was doing. He lit the candles and nodded with satisfaction.

The other man watched him with a derisive scowl. "A man would think you were a miserable sodomite with those pretty ways of yours, Peddler," he said.

"Some of us are what they call civilized, Mr. Goodson," the Peddler told him. "My old mother was particular about serving tea. She had the idea that it was proof positive we were descended from angels rather than the much-lamented apes. 'I'm on the side of the angels,' she'd say, taking out the china teapot. She didn't have the pleasure of knowing you, of course, Mr. Goodson. You might have changed her mind for her. Cup of tea, Professor St. Ives? Rather later than is customary, but we make do in our crude way."

St. Ives saw no reason to answer.

"Ah, I forgot that you were bound hand and foot, Professor. Not at all conducive to holding a teacup. We might untie our captive friend's hands, Mr. Goodson. Loop a noose around his neck first, however. Then you can lead him into the trees so that he can relieve himself in Mother Nature's waterless closet. The tea should be steeping by the time you return. We'll give the Professor something more fortifying—a restful glass of brandy, perhaps."

"Get your old mother to lead him into the woods," Goodson told him, nearly spitting out the words. Then he stepped across to the short-legged table, picked up the entire cheese, and took a great bite out of it, spitting the chunk into his hand and setting the cheese back down. He stood there chewing like a cow and glaring at the Peddler, who calmly removed a long clasp knife from his pocket, opened it, and sliced off the ruined corner of the cheese, which he flung over his shoulder. He flipped the open knife neatly into the air, moonlight glinting off the blade, and let it fall onto the table, where it stuck quivering.

"The Doctor would particularly appreciate your cooperation, Mr. Goodson. Indeed he would. He's a generous man, the Doctor—a generous man. No one moreso when good work's been done." The Peddler looked steadily at Goodson, who seemed to be reconsidering his ways. After a moment he swallowed what he was chewing and walked unhappily to the wagon, where he drew out a length of rope. His arm being in a sling, he awkwardly tied a slipknot into the end of it and then stepped across and dropped the loop over St. Ives's head before drawing the noose tight. Then he untied the Professor's hands, all the time staring into his face with a dark look.

"Up you go, cully," he said, hauling on the rope, and St. Ives had to scramble to his feet to avoid strangling. For all that, he was grateful enough for the short jaunt into the trees, and for more reasons than one. He looked out for Mr. Goodson to let his guard down, and he meant to cause him some real harm before the Peddler could join the fray. But the man had the rope wrapped half a dozen times around his good hand, and would without a doubt keep St. Ives on a long tether, pulling him taut at the first hint of a false move. With his feet hobbled, the Professor would have little chance of prevailing, but even so, he watched for his chance, determining to force the issue while the odds were close to even.

When they returned to the clearing again, the Peddler was standing at the wagon, pouring brandy into a cup. He nodded cheerfully at St. Ives. "Night-cap, Professor? Best you drink it while your hands are free. There's more dignity in it."

Clearly the question was meant as a command, and St. Ives took the cup as if he were happy to oblige, tasting the brandy before consuming it, the bitter flavor of chloral nearly making him spit. "Cheers," he said, and he pitched the brandy into the Peddler's face, spun around so that he was facing Goodson, and grabbed the line, yanking Goodson forward and off balance, slamming him on the nose with his knee, hard enough so that the man's head snapped back and he fell, the rope still wrapped around his hand. St. Ives was dragged forward, despite yanking savagely to free himself. The Peddler's arms wrapped around his chest just then, and he was lifted bodily off the ground, getting in one last boot-heel blow that caught Goodson in the forehead.

Goodson got up more slowly the second time, blood flowing from his nose. "Hold him still, Peddler," he said. Securing the coil of rope even more tightly around his hand, he drew back his arm and hit the Professor savagely on the cheek, the rope cutting into his flesh. He would have struck him again if the Peddler hadn't turned away.

"Fetch the funnel," the Peddler told him brusquely. "Give the rope to me." He set St. Ives down, took the line from Goodson, and quickly tied St. Ives's hands behind him again, so that his hands were tethered to his neck now. He pushed him back toward the bed of the wagon, still squinting his eyes against the sting of the brandy that St. Ives had flung into his face. "You'd best sit down of your own accord, Professor, or I'll let Goodson have his way with you. That's it. Now lie down on the straw there. He bound the Professor's feet tightly now, doing a neat job of it, then walked over to where the cup had landed in the dirt and picked it up. He took a satchel from Goodson, from which he removed a bottle of French brandy, followed by another small bottle, clearly from a chemist's shop, and a funnel with a long tube. He knocked the cup against the side of the wagon by way of cleaning it, and then poured brandy into it along with a heavy dose of chloral. St. Ives lay there looking up at the moon again, weighing the odds without any real hope. Resistance was useless. Better to bide his time. When the Peddler told him to open his mouth, he did it. The Peddler was middling accurate with the funnel, sliding it neatly into the Professor's throat and pouring the contents of the cup into it, and even though the liquor bypassed his tongue, St. Ives nearly gagged on the fumy bitterness of the chloral.

The gate came back up, the canvas was drawn back across, and he found himself once again lying in darkness, his head throbbing with pain, listening as if from a great distance to the sounds roundabout, of night birds and teacups and the racket of the table being stowed. He moved his jaw, relieved that it wasn't broken despite the pain, but almost anxious now for the chloral to take effect. The wagon set out once again, and very soon the St. Ives was slipping into a drugged darkness, thinking with the last remnants of his waking mind that his companions were somewhere very nearby, that Alice was with them, safe.

Chapter 9

Dry Bones
and Clinkers

W E CAUGHT SIGHT OF Tubby's Uncle Gilbert's house when we were halfway up the yew alley—a vast sort of Georgian pile with three tiers of windows. The ground floor looked large enough to house a company of marines, and smoke billowed from the chimney, which was a happy sight. There was a pond, too, with the moon shining on it, and a boathouse and dock with a collection of rowing boats serried alongside. "Uncle Gilbert is a boatman of the first water," Tubby told us, laughing out loud at his own pitiful wordplay.

Barlow, Uncle Gilbert's butler, let us in with great haste, as if, impossibly, he had been expecting our arrival.

Uncle Gilbert himself met us in the vestibule, leading us into a stately, oak-paneled room with coffered ceilings and stained glass windows depicting knights and dragons. Hasbro himself sat in a chair, drinking whiskey out of a cut glass tumbler, and when he saw us his face fell. He couldn't help himself. He had been full of the same hope and unease that Tubby and I had felt waiting for the Tipper at the Inn at Blackboys: he had banked on the thin chance that St. Ives would be with us. But now hope was dashed, and you could see what was left of it in his eyes. That changed, however, when he saw Alice. Something good had come of the day after all. Hasbro looked done up, as if he had traveled night and day to rendezvous with us, which in fact he had, having come back down by rail on an express to Eastbourne and then back up again to Dicker, arriving only a half hour ago.

There arose a gleam of optimism in my own mind, for the company was gathered together at last, the elephant reassembled, the waiting mostly over. I'm told that it's common among soldiers and sailors to feel both a sensible fear and a fortifying elation before going into battle, and my own emotions confirmed it that night. There was a great fire of logs burning in the hearth, which was sizable enough so that a person might step into it without stooping, if one wanted to be roasted alive. There were oil lamps lit, and the room shone with a golden glow, our shadows leaping in the firelight. The walls were hung with paintings of birds and sailing ships. It struck me that I couldn't remember having been in a more pleasant room with better companions—if only St. Ives were there. Already I was fond of Uncle Gilbert, who might have been Tubby's older twin, if that were possible, but with his hair disappeared except upon the sides, where it stuck out in tufts. The old man was in a high state of pleasure and surprise at Tubby's arrival, for he had himself been made uneasy by Hasbro's revelations. His pleasure was heightened considerably when he got a good look at Alice.

"Ravished, my dear," he said, bowing like a courtier and kissing her hand. "Simply ravished. You're a very diamond alongside these two lumps of coal." He gestured at Tubby and I. Then he shook my hand heartily, apologized for having called me a lump of coal, compelled me to admit to the truth of the insult, and then apologized again for having nothing but dry bones and clinkers to feed us. If he had known for certain that we were coming, he said, he would have slaughtered the fatted calf.

Barlow hauled me away at that point to see to my arm, which needed a proper cleaning and bandaging. He gave me one of his own shirts, my own being a bloody ruin, and he took my coat away with him to see whether Mrs. Barlow could put it right. Mrs. Barlow was at that moment apparently looking after Alice's needs. We were being looked after on all sides. I had the distinct notion that the earth was growing steadier on its axis after having been tilted this way and that for the past weeks.

I found my companions in the dining hall where they were just then sitting down to gnaw on the bones and clinkers, which turned out to be bangers and mash running with butter and gravy, cold pheasant, cheese and bread, and bottles of good burgundy. Barlow had already taken the corks out of three of the bottles, and the glasses stood full. You can imagine that we fell upon the food and drink like savages, Alice included, pausing only to answer Uncle Gilbert's myriad questions. He cocked his head at what we had to say, nodding seriously, cursing the man who had hit me on the head, astonished at the machinations of Ignacio Narbondo, who, he insisted, needed a good horsewhipping before he was bunged up in an empty keg with a rabid stoat and set adrift. He knew the Tipper, he said, from his hunting forays around Blackboys. Gibbet bait, he was. Vermin. A worm. Gutter filth. "We'll settle him," he told me, nodding heartily and tipping me a wink. "We'll hand him his head in a bucket." He seemed to be as worried for the Professor's health as we were, as if the two of them were old friends.

His use of the word "we" made me uneasy. I mentioned to him that we would be out of his way before dawn, which meant getting precious little sleep....

"Of course I'll come along," he said. "You'll need another stout hand when you beard these rogues." He stood up from his chair and crossed to the wall, where he took down a saber, cutting at the air with it and skipping toward a great, mullioned, oak chest full of crystal objects as if to hack it to pieces. I thought of Tubby beheading the stuffed boar in the Explorers Club. I was fond of Uncle Gilbert, as I said, but he was distinctly excitable. My refusing him outright, however, wouldn't have been gentlemanly, so I rather hoped that Tubby would come up with something to put him off the scent.

"You knew the Earl of Hamsters, didn't you Uncle?" Tubby asked as Barlow poured more wine into our glasses.

"Lord Busby, do you mean? I did indeed know him. We were at Cambridge together, you know, before we were sent down over a misunderstanding involving the fairer sex, ha ha. Pardon me," he said to Alice, "not half so fair as you, my dear. Anyway, I regretted it immensely, of course, but I mend quickly, and I was never any kind of scholar. I'm afraid it went ill for poor Busby, who was a frightfully sensitive man. Every small insult struck the man like a blow. The press made game of him, with the Earl of Hamsters comments, although he did have capacious cheeks. He had a trick of packing them full of walnut halves and then eating them one by one when we were in chapel. He saw nothing humorous in it, do you see. He simply didn't have to share them with the rest of us that way, or crack the nuts during sermon. Poor Busby had a run of ill luck after the scandal, and became a variety of scientific hermit. I felt badly when I read that he'd been murdered. What has he to do with our mission?"

I told him what I knew—about the Prussians, about Busby's experimental rays that were said to be impervious to the horizon and therefore monumentally dangerous, about the man's palpable fear when I met him, like a mouse expecting the imminent arrival of a snake. At that time he had been holed up in the top floor of a hotel on the hillside looking down on Scarborough Bay. It was a den of prostitutes and panel thieves, but he was attracted to the hidden passages. Everything in his laboratory was set up on an ingenious scaffolding of stout wooden crates, and could be packed up and spirited away on the instant.

I had witnessed the workings of the sapphire ray on that occasion—a propulsion ray generated by a device that Busby referred to as a 'transmuting lamp.' Light bounced around inside a cylinder containing the sapphire until it was released as a narrow stream of blue light— 'disciplined radiation,' as Busby would have it, although the phrase conveyed little meaning to my mind. The ray had sent a glass paperweight hurtling from where it sat on a table in front of the lamp, out through the open window and down into the sea. It plunged into the depths without so much as a visible splash, and was (for all I know) driven into the sea floor. The crystal structure of the sapphire was destroyed in the process, broken down, Busby told us, by 'imperfect hydrothermal synthesis,' although why the phrase has lingered in my mind I can't tell you. Mother nature's stones, to put it simply, were of inferior quality. It had been a costly little experiment (the expense apparently borne by the Prussians) and one that quite surprised the Professor. I didn't have the scientific wit to be surprised by it.

We agreed to meet again the following day. St. Ives, I believe, wanted to confront him on this issue of the Prussians, to talk sense, as they say, but Busby, perhaps anticipating some such thing, was gone from the hotel, lock, stock, and barrel when we returned. I was entirely ignorant of Busby's having entrusted St. Ives with the fortified emerald, and quite rightly. It was a monstrous thing in every sense of the word, a thing best kept secret. A short time later St. Ives and I found Busby dead in the upper deck of a folly tower in North Kent.

Uncle Gilbert shook his head in both sadness and astonishment. But he was as keen as a schoolboy to know about the emerald, and his eyes grew wide when Hasbro drew it out of a drawstring bag and set it on the table. It was a vast thing, and I say that as a man who himself came into the possession of an enormous emerald some few years back, which I've set into a broach as a wedding gift for Dorothy Keeble, my intended. Busby's manufactured emerald dwarfed my own. It fit neatly into the palm of Hasbro's hand, but only just. It was oddly flattened and faceted, evidently not cut for beauty's sake. There was something about it that was almost malignant, like a poisonous toad, or the proverbial ill wind that blows no good. Alice, I noticed, didn't care to look at it. Hasbro slipped it back into its bag.

"What can you tell us of the lighthouse, Uncle?" Tubby asked, gnawing on a pheasant bone.

"That it's a damned treacherous light," he said. "Hard to see. It's on the bluff, invisible when you're coming down from Eastbourne 'till you sail halfway around Beachy Head. In a sea mist, you don't know where you are. Captain Sawney was the keeper until recently. Drunk as a lord most of the time and asleep the rest, but he kept the lights topped off with oil and his wicks trimmed. You'd think he'd have fallen downstairs hauling oil up to the light or cleaning the blasted glass, but he didn't, the poor sod. He walked off the cliff one night in a mist. They went out to look because the light went dark for want of oil and found the Captain on the rocks below with his head bashed in, the crabs eating him. There's nothing on the beach below the headland but a ledge of shattered chalk. It comes down, you know, great masses of it some years."

"Uncle Gilbert knew Cap'n Sawney on account of the birding," Tubby said. "Beachy Head is a famous place for birds."

"Quite right," Uncle Gilbert said. "There's a sort of cow path that winds around from East Dean. First rate birding on the South Downs and along the cliffs. Eagle owls, long ears, whooper swans, merlin. A blind man could see two-dozen varieties in a day with half an eye open. Captain Sawney kept a log, pages and pages of observations. God knows what came of it. Used to wrap fish, probably."

"There's a new keeper, then?" Hasbro asked.

"Some three months or more. I've been down that way twice now that the weather's warmed up, taking a turn on the Downs with the binocle, but the new man won't come down. Captain Sawney always liked a chat. It gave him a chance for a whet, you see. Didn't matter what time of day. He'd bring the bottle and two glasses down with him. I'd sometimes haul along a fresh bottle myself and leave it with him in order to buy my round. If there was weather, I'd go up for the view. Many's the time we watched ships beating up the Channel in a storm. He always wanted to know what I'd seen in the birding line, and if there was anything new. He was fond of owls...."

His voice fell, and he saw something in our faces now. "They murdered him?" he asked after a silent moment. "He didn't fall? He was *pushed*?"

"Quite likely," Alice said. "I'm sorry."

"Then this new man...he's in league with your Dr. Narbondo? They put their own man in?" He didn't wait for an answer, but nodded darkly. He looked at his hands, opening and closing them. "It's late," he said, all the vigor gone out of his voice. "I want some rest. I suggest that we lay things out in the morning. I've an idea of how we might come at them." He nodded decisively. "We'll learn 'em," he said. "See if we don't."

The pheasant had been reduced to a skeleton, the wine drank, and the cheese and bread lay in a general ruin. Uncle Gilbert was quite right. There was nothing left to be said that would do us half so much good as a few hours of restorative sleep. As I rose from the table I wondered what "come at them" might mean, and what Uncle Gilbert intended to learn them.

Chapter 10

Go On
or Go Back

MORNING FOUND US ON the Downs, or at least it found three of us there, Alice, Hasbro, and I, hidden in the shrubbery that covered the hilltop just west of the light, eating sandwiches out of a basket put up by Barlow and drinking tea out of an ingenious traveling teapot. There was the twitter of birds and the morning sun through the leaves, and away off shore a schooner ghosted along, appearing and disappearing through a rising sea mist.

I watched the lighthouse through a pair of Uncle Gilbert's birding glasses. Five minutes ago a heavy, large man, most likely the keeper, had stepped out onto the encircling balcony carrying a telescope to take a look over the Downs as if he anticipated someone's arrival. There was smoke rising from the chimney of the attached cottage, and a light beyond the window—someone else waiting inside, perhaps. Maybe several someones, unless the keeper kept lamps burning even while he was out. He had lamp oil to spare, certainly.

White mist drifted through on the breeze off the Channel, obscuring the lighthouse and the edge of the cliffs now. When it cleared, Tubby and Uncle Gilbert appeared, coming along the path from the direction of Eastbourne like Tweedle-dee and Tweedle-dum. Tubby used his black-thorn as a walking stick and Uncle Gilbert leaned on what I knew to be a sword cane, and not one of the cheap variet-ies made for show. This one had an edge on it and a certain amount of heft. Both men wore walking togs and carried birding glasses, the very image of well fed amateur natural-ists taking advantage of the morning quiet. Uncle Gilbert stopped in his tracks, pointed skyward, clapped his glasses to his eyes, and watched a falcon turning in a great circle, drifting away northward. Tubby wrote what appeared to be an observation into a small notebook. A curtain of mist drifted between us again, and for a moment I saw noth-ing. When it cleared, they were halfway along the path to the lighthouse itself, Uncle Gilbert pointing up at the light, then at the schooner out in the Channel, apparently explaining nautical arcana to his nephew.

The plan proposed by Uncle Gilbert was simple: he and Tubby would chat up the lighthouse keeper on the off chance that he would let them take a look upstairs. Uncle Gilbert wasn't a stranger to the Downs, after all—the keeper would suspect nothing. A jolly peek at the light wasn't much to ask. The man's allowing it wouldn't demonstrate his innocence, but we would know something about the location of Busby's lamp, at least in the negative. And if the keeper wasn't amenable? They would persuade him, Uncle Gilbert had said, laughing at the word. But the whole thing must be done by eleven o'clock if Hasbro was to heed the ransom demand and give up the emerald at the lighthouse. If they failed to produce St. Ives, then he would give up nothing, but would look to his pistol.

Tubby knocked on the door of the cottage now, and they stood waiting. Then he knocked on it again, with his stick this time, and they stepped back in anticipation. But the door remained shut, the window curtains still, the smoke tumbling up out of the chimney. They went on around to the door of the lighthouse and treated it in a similar fashion, stepping back so as not to crowd the keeper if he opened it, which he did, directly.

He was a swarthy, heavy man in a Leibnitz cap. I could see through the glasses that he was scowling, as if he had perhaps been awakened by their racket. Uncle Gilbert gestured at the Downs, perhaps explaining what the two of them were up to, and then up at the light. The keeper shook his head, seemed to utter something final, and stepped back inside, shutting the door after him. Tubby turned as if to walk away, but Uncle Gilbert didn't follow. He stood looking at the door, studying it, and then smote it hard several times, the handle of the sword cane held in his fist. The sound of the knocking reached us an instant later.

"Here's trouble," I said to Alice and Hasbro, who could see well enough what I meant. Uncle Gilbert held the cane before him now, his left hand on the scabbard, his right gripping the hilt. "We'll have to act if we lose sight of them in the fog," I said, "or if that cottage door opens."

"Not the three of us," Hasbro put in. "I have a revolver, after all. I'll lend them a hand, but you two should remain hidden."

"Yes," Alice said.

Hasbro removed the velvet bag from his pocket, drew out the emerald, and sank it in the teapot, fastening down the lid afterward. "No use taking it into the fray," he said.

Tubby turned now and said something to Uncle Gilbert, apparently trying to draw him away. Our battle, after all, wasn't with the lighthouse keeper, although perhaps Uncle Gilbert's was. Perhaps he meant to strike a blow on behalf of Captain Sawney.

The lighthouse door swung open again, and the keeper strode out onto the little paved porch, closing the door behind him. He held a belaying pin in his fist. Tubby walked back toward them, stepping behind his uncle, who was talking and gesturing, his voice rising. The keeper pointed with the pin, as if telling them to clear out. Then a wisp of fog blew through, and when it dissipated everything had changed. Uncle Gilbert was sprawled on the ground, on his back like an overturned tortoise, and Tubby had drawn the blackthorn stick back to strike a blow. There was incoherent shouting as the keeper rushed at Tubby, ducking under the blackthorn. The keeper clipped Tubby on the side of the head with the belaying pin, but Uncle Gilbert had crawled to his knees by then, blood running from a wound on his forehead, and he delivered the keeper a great blow on the back of the head with the sheathed sword. And thank God it was sheathed, because if it had not been the man's head would have been split like a melon, and although dead men tell no tales, as they say, there's no virtue in collecting specimens.

The keeper pitched forward, and Uncle Gilbert struck him again, hard, and snatched the cane back for the third blow, the sheath flying off the blade now, end over end. Tubby parried the sword blow with the blackthorn to save his uncle from the gallows, but the keeper scrambled to his feet more nimbly than I would have thought possible and attempted to hit Tubby another savage blow on the side of the head, although it caught him on the shoulder as Tubby twisted away. Hasbro was up and out of the blind now, running down the slope toward the lighthouse, vanishing in the rising fog, which sailed through heavier this time. Right before the curtain closed, however, I saw the door of the cottage fly open, and a man—a small man—come out at a dead run. It was the Tipper, wearing his slouch hat, turning up like a bad penny. I scanned the downs with the glasses, trying to sort things out but hampered by the wall of mist. Then I saw him briefly at the very edge of the precipice, where he disappeared like a goblin over the ledge as if he meant to scramble down the face of Beachy Head and swim across the Channel to France.

"I'm following him!" I said to Alice, which would be senseless blather if she hadn't seen the Tipper emerge from the cottage. I crawled out the back of the copse to open ground and ran toward the cliff, slowing down when I neared the edge, wary of suffering the fate of Captain Sawney. I looked back toward the lighthouse but made out nothing, although I could dimly hear the sounds of the struggle. I could see perhaps thirty feet downward through the mist, and straightaway spotted the shadowy form of the Tipper as he made his way along what was apparently a narrow trail cut into the chalk. From far below came the muffled sound of the swell washing in over the rocky beach, but I couldn't see it, which was just as well, because I meant to follow the Tipper downward, and I wasn't keen on the view.

It was then that I saw a length of three-inch line below and to the right, the color of the chalk of the cliffs and nearly invisible. It was affixed to a heavy iron ring-and-bolt driven into the rock, a holdfast that allowed for a person to climb downward in comparative safety. It had been there for some time, for it was weather-frayed and there was rust on the bolt. I waited until the Tipper was safely out of sight, and then stepped onto the narrow trail, which was steep, but fortunately clear of loose debris. I didn't tarry, but intended to remain just out of sight in the fog, which meant keeping one eye on what I was doing and another farther down the path in case the Tipper came into view.

I scuttled down sideways, hanging on to the rope carefully, all the time watching and listening for the Tipper. I had made my way perhaps fifty feet from the top of the precipice, when the wind gusted and the fog cleared utterly. I found myself looking down the edge of the cliff, which was unnervingly sheer, the sea moving over the shingle nearly five hundred feet below. My head spun with sudden vertigo when I saw that moving water, and I threw myself into a crouch against the cliff face, grasping the hand-line and closing my eyes. When I opened them again, the fit having passed, the Tipper was gone, although he might still be somewhere on the trail farther below, hidden by an outcropping.

I heard a scrabbling sound above me, and there was Alice, coming along downward with considerably more grace and agility than I had shown. She clutched her dress out of the way with one hand and held onto the line with the other, and within moments she stood beside me. "He's vanished," she said, apparently referring to the Tipper. "I assumed you meant to follow him, so I decided to do the same. He'll lead us to Langdon."

"What of the emerald?" I asked.

"The emerald doesn't interest me, Jack. It only interests Doctor Narbondo. My husband is my sole interest, but he doesn't interest Narbondo at all, except as a means to an end. When the end is achieved…" She shrugged, looking out over the sea as if St. Ives were somewhere beyond the horizon.

"We'll find him," I said, starting downward again while the weather was clear. The trail doubled back toward the east, although some distance ahead it was apparently blocked by a great slab of chalk that had slipped from above and which stood precariously among a litter of boulders. The handhold ended there, bolted to the slab. Perhaps it started up again beyond. If the Tipper had seen us above him when the fog lifted, he might easily be waiting for us, hiding behind the great rock. It would be a simple thing for him to reach out and give us a hearty push when we edged around it, and us with nothing to hold onto but sea air.

But Alice made it clear that it was go on or go back for the two of us, and she was clearly in no mood to go back. We approached the great slab warily. The trail was littered with a scree of chalk and flint now, which chattered away downward with each step. The Tipper would certainly hear us approaching if he were hidden up ahead. But now that we were closer, I couldn't for the life of me see how he could have climbed past the slab, unless he were some variety of ape, for it thrust out over the ledge that it stood on, almost in defiance of gravity, the cliff face angling inward below it.

It wasn't until we were two or three steps from it that we saw the dark crack of the cavern mouth, which would be completely hidden from above and below both. It lay behind the slab itself. From out to sea, it would appear to be merely a long shadow cast by the slab and the overhanging cliff. But it was a cave mouth right enough, and we stood looking into the dark interior in utter silence, listening hard but hearing nothing but the calling of gulls and the sighing of the ocean below.

Chapter 11

Uncle Gilbert Parlays with the Lighthouse Keeper

THE BLOW THAT FELLED Tubby was the last that the keeper would strike, for as soon as Tubby no longer stood in the way, Uncle Gilbert stepped forward and skewered the man in the shoulder, wrenching out the sword and drawing it back, watching the belaying pin clatter to the paving stones. The keeper's face had a stupefied look on it, his doom writ plainly on Gilbert's face.

"Greetings from Captain Sawney!" the old man shouted, and swung the sword at the keeper's neck, lunging forward to throw his vast weight into the blow. But the keeper wisely dropped to the stones, sitting down and rolling sideways, and the sword passed harmlessly through the air, spinning Uncle Gilbert half around. The keeper scrambled away crablike, lurching to his feet and grasping his shoulder, backing away onto the meadow and turning to run before the old man was after him again.

It was then that Hasbro loomed up out of the fog, holding the pistol. Tubby was just then coming round, his face awash with gore, as was Uncle Gilbert's, who stood there panting for breath, his chest heaving with exertion. After a moment he walked the several steps to the fallen sheath and once again turned his sword into a cane. Tubby heaved himself up with an effort, and they made their way to the cottage, the door standing open now.

"By God someone's come out of here while we were busy," Tubby said. "He must have been hidden by this bloody fog."

"Perhaps," replied Hasbro, who looked into the interior warily, his pistol at the ready as they entered. It was a single, open room, with a fireplace dead center in the opposite wall, burned-down logs still aglow. A bedchamber stood off to the side, built as an open, lean-to closet with a curtain half drawn across it and a long cord hanging down alongside to tie it back. The door of a privy opened into a second closet, the door ajar, revealing that the small room was empty. There was a narrow dining table with a pair of chairs standing beneath a window looking east, an upholstered chair near the hearth, and a sideboard with plates and cups that stood beside an iron stove. A bowl and pitcher sat on a three-legged table, with a towel hanging alongside. Shoved into a corner sat several open wooden crates stuffed with excelsior. Nondescript pieces of brass and iron poked out of the stuffing.

"There's your evidence," said Uncle Gilbert nodding at the crates. "Our man here is an assassin, or I'm King George."

Hasbro stepped across to the curtain that half-hid the bedchamber, drawing it back slowly, his pistol at the ready. No one was there. Someone had been in the cottage earlier, but whoever it was had fled like a coward rather than to take the keeper's side in the battle.

"Take a seat in that chair, my good fellow," Tubby said, gesturing at the stuffed chair with his blackthorn. The keeper sat down heavily, still holding his shoulder, although there was no longer any apparent flow of blood.

Hasbro put away his pistol in order to take a look into the top crate, which yielded short lengths of glass and metal pipe of various dimensions and what appeared to be a three-sided mirror that filled the palm of his hand. The words "Exeter Fabricators" were burned into the wooden slats of the crate.

"That's as has to do with the light up topside," the keeper said, jerking his head upward. "Property of the Crown."

"Property of Lord Busby if you ask me," Uncle Gilbert said. "But we'll get to the bottom of it in due course."

Hasbro nodded. "Indeed," he said. "I'll just be off, then, if you gentlemen have everything in order. My companions will be wondering what I'm about. You'll want to take a look at the light, perhaps? If the device is still there, you'll do well to dismantle it, but I don't hold out much hope. The rendezvous, then?"

"Just so," Tubby said. "We'll be out of the way when the time comes."

With that Hasbro stepped through the door and disappeared into the mist.

Uncle Gilbert looked out after him for a moment and then closed the door quietly. "We both need a swab, Tubby," he said, and he walked to the three-legged table, poured water into the basin, and dipped the towel into the water, wiping the drying blood off his face while peering into a mirror that hung on the wall. Tubby stood by, ready to cave in the keeper's skull with the blackthorn if the man invited it. Then they traded places and Tubby washed himself, the keeper looking back and forth nervously, first at one and then the other.

"Do you mind if a man has a pipe of tobacco?" he asked.

"Which man would that be?" Uncle Gilbert said to him. "There are only two of us here, and neither of us has the habit."

The keeper looked at him blankly. "I just thought I might…"

"Ah!" Uncle Gilbert said, leaning heavily on his cane. "Your use of the word 'man' confounded me. But I suppose that even a dull-witted reptile like yourself might have learned to stuff a pipe. By all means, then."

The keeper removed a briar from his coat pocket, all the while looking nervously at Uncle Gilbert. The old man's face was a grimacing mask as he watched the keeper load tobacco into the bowl and tamp it down with a ten penny nail, setting the pipe between his teeth and producing a Lucifer match from his vest. He lit the match on his shoe sole and put it to his pipe. Uncle Gilbert whipped the sword cane upward then, knocking the pipe out of the man's mouth. It clattered away onto the floor, spinning to a stop near Tubby's foot. Tubby picked up his blackthorn and smashed the heavy end against the pipe, shattering the bowl into pieces and cracking off the stem. "It'll draw like a chimney now," Tubby said, nodding heartily and hanging the towel on its hook.

"Knock him into the Channel if he moves," Uncle Gilbert said. With that he strode toward the bedchamber, unsheathed his sword, and hacked through the cords that hung next to the curtain. He returned with the pieces and set about tying the keeper into the chair, the man dead silent, his eyes moving from Tubby to Uncle Gilbert and back again, full of loathing and fear.

"Be a good lad and stoke up that fire, Tubby," Uncle Gilbert said heartily. "We'll want it as hot as the hinges of Hades after we've had a look upstairs at that light. We'll see whether our fellow here can sing." He grinned into the keeper's face. Tubby piled split logs onto the dog grate and the fire swept up around it, throwing sparks up the chimney. The two men filed out through the door onto the meadow again, hurrying around to the lighthouse door and stepping inside the vestibule.

Several more of Busby's crates lay on the floor, empty but for tangles of excelsior. The spiral stairs wound away upward, and the two set out, climbing slowly, Uncle Gilbert wheezing but coming along manfully. The great lights burned with good lengths of wick, the oil recently topped off. There was a broad balcony that ran around the outside, and they stepped out onto it, seeing immediately that a platform had been set up there in the open air, bolted to the railing for the sake of stability. Atop the platform stood what appeared to be a large and very finely calibrated compass, vast as a barrow wheel, with a rotating face. There was a second platform fixed above it, studded with bolts and with a confusion of

gears and a crank for the purpose of tilting and swivel-
ing. The second platform was empty. But the debris in
the crates downstairs had made the thing clear: Busby's
ray-producing lamp had almost certainly been moored
to this second platform, where it could be aimed like a
precisely-manipulated cannon.

They descended the stairs and went out onto the
meadow again, the spring sun having melted away most
of the fog now. The morning was wearing on. Uncle
Gilbert threw the cottage door open in order to have a
telling effect on the lighthouse keeper, who back pedaled
with his feet, as if to scurry out of range.

"Thrust that poker into the fire, Tubby!" Uncle
Gilbert cried. "We'll melt his eyeballs out like jellies, the
lying dog!" He laughed hard into the keeper's face, then
stood back and regarded him through squinted eyes.
"Say your prayers, my man, if you have any to say. It
was you who murdered Captain Sawney. You'll admit it
before we're done with you."

"Captain bloody *Sawney*?" the man said. "I didn't
know the man. You're daft!"

"He was your predecessor, you lying toad!" Uncle
Gilbert said. "The man you threw down the cliff."

"*Down the cliff?* I was sent out by Trinity House, by
God! I was second man at the Dover light, and they sent
an agent up from Eastbourne to fetch me. I was told that

Cap'n Sawney had come a purler off the top of the Head, and I was filling in, temporary like, till I passed the trial. I swear on my old mother's grave!"

"What's your name, then?" Uncle Gilbert asked, abruptly pleasant and smiling.

"Stoddard. Billy Stoddard, your honor."

"Billy, is it? Sounds like a name for one of the lads, doesn't it? Fancy a murderer with a pleasant name like Billy. Scarcely stands to reason. How's that poker coming along, Nephew? Hot?"

"Red hot, I should think," Tubby said, holding up the glowing iron.

"Isn't that grand! We'll start with his eyeballs then. He's got two of them. When the first one bursts it'll give him a chance to consider his ways, like the Old Book advises. Ever see a sheep's eyeball burst when the head's on the boil, Billy?"

The man sat gaping at him.

"It swells up first, you see, to twice the size. Then it pops right out of the socket and splits open like a banger on a griddle. The French are fond of an eyeball. They eat them with periwinkle forks. I'm told that a well-turned sheep's eyeball has the consistency of mayonnaise, but a distinctly muttony flavor, which doesn't surprise one. I'll take it now, nephew, before it cools down. We'll want the full sizzle."

Tubby handed it over gingerly, more than slightly ill at ease. Uncle Gilbert seemed to have come unhinged—an unfortunate state of affairs for the keeper.

"Clutch a handful of his hair, Tubby, and hold fast," the old man said. "He'll make a mighty by-God effort to fly when the poker slides in past the eyeball. It'll take all your strength. If he pulls away, though, it'll fry his brainpan, and he'll be no good to us nor anyone else, the poor sod."

Tubby did as he was told. If Uncle Gilbert had gone off his chump and actually meant to burn the man's eyes out, he would pull the keeper over backward in the chair....

Squinting at the smoking end of the poker, the old man inched it toward the keeper's face, regarding him with a wide-eyed, sideways stare as if concentrating utterly on his task. "Hold him still now!" he cried.

Tubby held on tightly, bracing the toe of his boot against the chair leg.

The keeper shut his eyes tight and cringed away as best he could. "It's better to save the eyelid, Billy," Uncle Gilbert shouted into his face. "But if you don't care for it, it's not my lookout. Latch on, now, Tubby! His time has come!"

"Jesus, Mary, and Joseph!" the keeper shouted, and then began to gag, his head rotating on his neck as if he were augering a hole in the sky.

"I believe he's swallowed his tongue," Uncle Gilbert said matter-of-factly. He handed the poker to Tubby with instructions to put it back into the fire. The keeper looked up now, one eye open, gasping for air. "Now, my man, what do you know of the death of Captain Sawney? Mark me well, you'll by-God tell us or you'll go out eyeless onto the Downs like a beggar man!"

"Not a bloody damned thing, mate," the keeper gasped out. "I swear to you. They told me that he'd gone off the top of Beachy Head. Trinity House give me a trial. Half a year at half keeper's pay and a tight-knit little cottage—better than second man at Dover, says I, and down I come with my kit."

"And yet here you are tied into a chair, Billy, close as a toucher to losing your eyeballs and the good Lord knows what all else. You assaulted the two of us on the porch outside when we asked you a civil question, and you've got these wooden crates full of Lord Busby's goods. It doesn't stand to reason that you're innocent, Billy."

"*Lord Busby!* I don't know him neither. And they ain't mine, them crates. Them others brought that trash round, don't you see? Them damned scientists. They set up shop up in the lighthouse. They give me a few quid, maybe, to watch out, but murder...? I swear to God it ain't in me to kill a man."

"You gave it a try not long back when you laid us both out with that belaying pin," Uncle Gilbert said.

"You was a-beating of me!"

"Who was in the cottage, then?" Tubby asked.

"A bloke. Just a bloke. One of them as I told you."

"What sort of bloke? What's his name? Quick-like!"

"The Tipper they call him. He's a man does odd jobs for the others."

"Which others would that be, Billy?" Uncle Gilbert asked.

"There's three that I knows of besides the Doctor, him what set up the device."

"The Doctor is it?" asked Tubby. "The Doctor came and went? Left you to mind the shop?"

"Just so. Past few days."

"They must be bivouacked somewhere nearby then."

"Eastbourne, I'd think…" the keeper started to say, but Uncle Gilbert shook his head into the man's face to stop him.

"It won't do, Billy. They didn't flog up and down from Eastbourne. It doesn't make sense. I don't call it a *damned* lie that you're telling us, but it's some such." He shook his head tiredly. "Well, as the poet said, red-hot pokers doth make falsettos of us all."

"He'll *do* for me, don't you see!"

"*Who* will, Billy?"

"*The bleeding Doctor.* You don't know him. I can see that. If you knew him you wouldn't be using me so. You'd ken what I'm up against."

"I ken it well," Uncle Gilbert said. "I can see it with my own eyes. You're tied into a chair and I'm about to burn your deadlights out. What's not to ken? But you've already peached on the Doctor, don't you see, Billy? He'll know you've been a-talking with us. There's precious little the Doctor doesn't know. If I were you I'd say what *I* know and skedaddle. They're always looking for hands on the docks in Eastbourne. A two-year cruise might answer. Difficult for a blind man to find a berth, though...."

"By God that's *just* what I'll do," the keeper cried. "I don't half like this work, and I don't half like the Doctor. Ask me a question and I'll tell you fair, but I didn't kill no Captain Sawney."

"Where's the Doctor's lamp, then? Quick."

"They took it away. Middle of last night it was. Experiment was finished, they said. They cleared out, the lot of them. Then the Tipper, he showed up two hours ago and said he was done up, said he would take a bit of a nap, and I let him have his way. No harm in a nap."

"Where are they, then? Where'd they clear out *to*? No nonsense now. Tell us and you walk away whole."

The keeper sat thinking for a moment, as if making up his mind, and then he began to speak.

Chapter 12

The Window
on the World

W E WAITED, STANDING THERE on the face of the cliff, not talking, but listening. Certainly the Tipper had slipped into the cavern and vanished. He had fled the lighthouse to avoid running afoul of Tubby, and it was unlikely that he thought to lure us into the darkness to waylay us, because he didn't know we were there. I looked at my watch, surprised to see that the morning had nearly flown. It was half ten o'clock—another thirty minutes until the rendezvous at the light. "Whither?" I asked.

"We'll give him another minute or two and then follow him into the cliffs," Alice said. "He'll lead us to something. It's our good luck that he ran off into the woods in Blackboys."

I hope so, I thought. "What about the others—Tubby and Uncle Gilbert?"

"They're grown men," she said. "They'll get along well enough."

Gulls wheeled around us, and small seabirds flew out of crannies in the chalk and flew back in again. Birds of prey rode effortlessly on the drafts rising from below. Uncle Gilbert could have named them all, no doubt. The sea wind blew ever more freshly, straight through one's clothing. To the west the Seven Sisters stretched away, and below us the swell washed in. On the horizon a low brown haze might have been the coast of France.

We slipped into the darkness of the cavern and waited again, allowing our eyes to grow accustomed to the twilight. We were in a high room—a sort of chalk rotunda with a window letting in sunlight high above, which illuminated a domed ceiling. As the moments passed I became aware of a general movement roundabout me, the cavern apparently alive with crawling and flying things. Moths of great size flitted through the air, and chitonous insects scurried away across the floor, which was littered with what were apparently bones, perhaps fossilized bones, and a rubble of flints and sea shells. Water dripped here and there from above, running in dark rivulets downhill along a dim passage, apparently along the edge of the cliff itself. Some forty or fifty feet farther another wash of sunlight shone through yet another window in the wall.

Alice set out across the cavern toward the passage, with me following as quietly as I could, although the rubble on the floor rattled and scraped as we trod on it. The second window stood at head-height, appearing to be a natural fissure in the rock. Someone had chiseled it larger, however, and the chalk was nearly white where it was newly exposed. The walls of the passage itself were gray, however, with black blotches and streaks of red, and here and there veins of quartz and flint. The stream ran heavier in its channel, fed by further streams where surface water filtered through from above, having dissolved the chalk over the long ages.

We passed into darkness, stepping into the surprisingly chill stream more than once and soaking our shoes, the passage leading ever downward, sometimes steeply. The air had grown stale, but I got a scent of salt air suddenly, and rounding a corner I saw another window, nearly level with the floor this time and providing scant illumination, but enough so that I could see that the passage turned again ahead, and then again after that. On we went, time ticking away. It seemed to me that we might easily have passed beyond Beachy Head proper, into one of the Seven Sisters, and that soon we would come level with the Channel itself if we continued downward at the current rate.

In time, however, the passage leveled off. We saw a tiny flame hovering in the darkness ahead of us, surrounded by a golden aura. When we drew near to it, I could see that it was a large lantern, sitting in a carved-out niche. It must have held a couple of pints of lamp oil, which meant that someone routinely filled it to keep it alight—someone who might be making his rounds at that very moment, lurking nearby. There was nothing for it, though, but to go on, ever on the watch for movement in the far shadows or for the sound of footsteps. Another lantern glowed beyond the first, and I could see that the floor of the cave had been swept clean now, as if we had arrived at a habitation. Chunks of chalk had been pushed up against the far wall in a heap, with a wheelbarrow upside-down atop it. On our right-hand side an arched doorway stood open, through which light glowed. Like the windows along the seaward passage, the doorway had apparently been enlarged, which accounted for the chalk pieces in the rubble heap. At first all was quiet, the air deathly still, and then there was the sound of movement, clearly coming from within the lighted room.

I shrugged at Alice and nodded at the doorway. She nodded back at me, and at once I stepped in front of her and walked silently forward. If one of us were going to stick our head into the lion's den, it would be me. I wafered myself against the wall, craning my neck to see past the edge of the door. What I saw was my own rather murky face looking out of what was apparently an illuminated mirror that framed the front of a wooden wardrobe cabinet.

I admit that the unexpected sight confounded me, although the confusion vanished when I saw that there was another face peering at me from out of the glass— the grimacing face of Dr. Ignacio Narbondo, who sat atop a wheeled stool, his back to the door. He regarded me without the least show of surprise. I gestured at Alice, still hidden behind me, waving her away, praying that she would vanish back into the darkness. Then I walked calmly into the Doctor's presence as if I had been invited.

I was aware in that moment of how few times I had actually set eyes on Narbondo, and then most often from a distance. He was one of those men who keep to the shadows, living in out-of-the-way places in the country-side, or inhabiting low dens deep in the rookeries of the Seven Dials or Limehouse. He was largely unknown to the police—the sort of evil genius whose machinations are carried out by men easily manipulated by greed or fear. He was gnome-like in feature, and middling small in stature, although he was rather stout and was as pale as a frog's belly. There was something bent about him—something you saw at once, or rather felt. I don't refer to his being a hunchback, which is neither here nor there, but to something hellish and inhuman in his demeanor, some fell presence that made him appear to be a leering devil. One could easily imagine Narbondo taking pleasure in flaying small animals, but the idea of his drinking a cup of tea or a pint of ale with any relish was impossible. A dog would cross the road to avoid him.

He sat there regarding me now, not seeming in the least unhappy to see me. "I'll show you a wonder, Mr. Owlesby," he said simply, gesturing at the mirror.

I realized then that the oil lamps that stood in niches around the circular room were unlit, and yet the room was illuminated with a pale glow, the light emanating from disks of glass set into the chalk of the ceiling, looking like full moons. Somehow he had contrived to pipe sunlight far back into the cliffs as if it were water. Aside from the stool and the cabinet that supported the large mirror, the room was empty of furnishings. Broad tubes, apparently made of copper, descended from the ceiling into the wooden closet, the door of which, as I said, was the mirror itself. In front of Narbondo stood a ship's wheel affixed to a complication of gears and levers that evidently worked whatever mechanical contrivance was housed in the wardrobe.

The reflection in the glass, as I said, was of inferior quality. My features were vague, and seemed almost to ripple, as if I were looking back through a haze of heat rising from hot summer pavement. But then I saw moving shapes in the glass, and my eyes looked to a point beyond the shimmering surface, where, to my vast amazement, there was a scenic view of the surface world—a ghostly view, as if some of its substance had evaporated during its journey through the periscope. I saw a line of trees that were certainly the edge of the South Downs woods, and below them, across an expanse of meadow, our own copse, where lay the emerald in the traveling teapot and my half-eaten sandwich. And out of that copse, as I stood there watching, strode Hasbro himself, just then putting his watch into his vest pocket.

Narbondo turned the ship's wheel, exactly as if he were navigating a vessel across the empty Downs, following Hasbro's progress. The lighthouse and cottage swung into view, and beyond them the edge of the cliffs and the sky over the Channel. Hasbro stopped before the door of the cottage, raised his hand, and knocked on it. The hour of the ransom was upon us. The door opened, although the dim interior hid whoever stood within. For a moment all was frozen. No doubt someone was speaking, but of course I could hear nothing. Then Hasbro took half a step backward, turned toward the cliffs, and toppled over slowly. A man stepped out of the interior of the lighthouse and stood for a moment looking down. He held a revolver in his hand. It was Sam Burke, the Peddler. He bent over, rifled Hasbro's pockets, and removed what he wanted. Hasbro shifted then, trying to sit up, and the Peddler drew back the revolver and clubbed him on the side of the head before dragging his now-limp body in through the door. After a time he stepped back out and closed the door behind him.

And then, strangely, he waved at me, or at us, very solemnly, before setting out across the Downs in the direction of the cliffs, disappearing out of the scene, which was now merely a picture postcard view of the Belle Tout Light. The horror of what I had witnessed was accentuated by its utter silence—a dumb show of viciousness.

"What do you think, Mr. Owlesby?" Narbondo said. "You've just witnessed what amounts to a small scientific miracle, given that you and I are three hundred feet beneath the earth's surface. It's the wonder of the ages, is it not? And all accomplished with mirrors, like a circus illusion."

I stared at him in stony silence, which he apparently took as an invitation to explain himself further.

"I envisioned a sort of Momus Glass," he said, "but looking outward and not inward. The mirror itself wasn't difficult to construct, but the necessity of tunneling through chalk was something else again. I contrived a mechanical mole to burrow to the surface, and then built a copper chimney set with highly polished mirrors of various shapes and magnifications. It's a toy, really. But one gets weary of spending time in caverns, you see, and longs for a view of the outside world. The sad case of Tennyson's Lady of Shallot comes to mind...."

"The Peddler knew he was being watched," I said. "Why did he wave at us? Was that a mere pleasantry? Mockery, perhaps?"

"It meant simply that he had done his duty."

"We had seen as much."

"No, we had not seen as much. What we saw was merely the initial step—the shooting of the man Hasbro. The Peddler was constrained from killing your man outright, but he could scarcely allow him his freedom. As you saw, he dragged him indoors, where he was to see to his wounds before binding him into a chair. Now mark this: in the room with him sits an infernal device with a simple clockwork mechanism. There is quite a lot of explosive, enough to demolish the lighthouse and to alter the contour of Beachy Head. If I'm at all unhappy with the quality of the emerald, we'll let your man sit there until the device detonates. Ideally he won't bleed to death in the mean time."

I turned on my heel and lunged through the door, possessed of a cold fury. There were tools atop the rubble pile. I would beat him to death with a shovel like the vermin that he was!

But two men stood without, and I nearly hurtled into them, one of them—the Tipper—tripping me up so that I sprawled on the ground. The other was a man I hadn't seen before. He wore his arm in a sling, and quickly I deduced that he must be none other than the railway thief. In his free hand he held a pistol. I found that I wasn't attracted to pistols, especially in the hands of my enemies. I stood up slowly, surreptitiously looking around, wondering about Alice, relieved that she was nowhere to be seen. The Tipper appeared to be amused to see me, no doubt full of hubris at having once again prevailed over me.

"That'll do, gents," Narbondo said. He lurked behind me in the open doorway, his face in shadow. "If you'll allow me to borrow your weapon, Mr. Goodson," he said, "I'll escort our bold Mr. Owlesby to the room where his companion is taking his ease, and the two of you can finish conveying our cargo to the ship. We sail with the tide."

Mr. Goodson did as he was told, and the two of them walked off silently. I was left alone with Narbondo, who gestured with the pistol, the two of us setting out at once along a down-sloping passage, its mouth nearly invisible in the heavy shadows. Soon, however, lantern light illuminated the passage, and I could see easily enough. This part of the caverns was apparently a warren of rooms and tunnels, most of them dark, although twice we passed lamp-lit rooms heaped with casks and crates, as if the place had been a smugglers' lair. It would have been vitally interesting at any other time, but my mind was fixed variously on Alice and on making a play for the pistol.

Narbondo followed behind me, fairly close. I could almost feel the weight of the pistol against the small of my back, as if it, too, emitted some sort of physical ray. I envisioned turning, batting away the hand that held the weapon, slamming the Doctor bodily into the wall. I determined to do it and steeled myself for the assault. But I had thought too long about it, for the tunnel steepened now, becoming a narrow stairway cut into the chalk. The cavern wall on the right abruptly disappeared, and we descended into a vast, open room, the floor a hundred or more feet below us, so that any quick, erratic movement might have precipitated me into the abyss.

Again sunlight shone through natural windows in the chalk walls high above. There was an updraft of air now, heavy with the smell of the ocean and sea wrack, and I heard what sounded like the relentless surging of the waves. I caught sight of birds winging across the open expanse, darting and flitting as if snatching insects out of the air. We were in a monumental sea cave, the floor of which was a pool of dark water. Small waves washed across the surface of the pool, breaking against tumbled rocks. Alongside a wooden dock lay Narbondo's submarine vessel, and even in the dim twilight of the cave I could see a glint of light from its portholes and the shadow of its dorsal fin. It seemed clear that Narbondo was waiting only on the fortified emerald in order to be underway, and when he gained his objective he would disappear into the vast oceans, surfacing at will to rain down literal madness on some unsuspecting corner of the world.

The flight of stairs ended on a natural outcropping of the chalk, chiseled flat to make a sort of landing some twenty feet in length and width. A second flight of stairs descended from the landing to the bottom of the sea cave, another fifty feet below. Immediately beside us stood wooden door, barred with a length of oak. On the door, hanging on pegs, were four of the Tipper's asbestos caps, looking incongruous in that vast, subterranean place.

"I'll ask you to step away from the door, Mr. Owlesby," Narbondo said, speaking in a polite tone that increased my desire to strangle him. "You have the look of a desperate man about you. If you'd like to hobnob with your friend the professor, you'd best don one of these admirable headpieces. If, on the other hand, you take it into your mind to bolt down the stairs, I might or might not shoot you in the back, but I can assure you that you'll next see your friend singing in the heavenly choir. And for goodness sake, keep that infernal device in mind. It's very much on the mind of that poor trussed up fellow topside. If all goes well, perhaps you'll have an opportunity to do the man the favor of saving his no doubt invaluable life. In short, the fate of your friends very much rests in your capable hands, so pray do not be foolhardy."

I stepped away, just as he asked, taking him entirely at his word. He removed one of the caps from its peg and tossed it to me. I put it on and watched as he tugged one tightly down over his ears, holding onto the pistol and gazing at me steadily, and all the time half smiling, as if he found the business slightly amusing. "I'll thank you to open the door and to step inside now," he said.

I dutifully lifted the bar out of its holdfasts, set it aside, and swung the door outward. Within lay a largish room. Again there was a window in the chalk, a stiff breeze from off the channel blowing through it, stirring the dust on the floor. On a wooden platform stood Busby's lamp, the lens shining mistily with a dim green glow. Behind it lay an array of jars and wires—the Bunsen battery that I had last seen in Busby's loft in Scarborough. Atop a small table were vials and bottles of various chemicals. To the left of the door a long sort of bench had been cut into the wall, and on it sat the open wooden coffin that I had seen in the photograph at the inn. St. Ives lay within it, his eyes closed, the lower half of the coffin lid fastened down. I could see movement behind his eyelids, as if he was dreaming, and his face was enlivened almost theatrically with rapidly altering emotions. His eyes jerked open and he uttered a quick gasp, and then they closed again, and his entire body seemed to twitch.

"Stand closer to your friend, if you will, Mr. Owlesby," Narbondo said. "It takes only one hand, you see, to manipulate the lever that increases the power of Busby's cleverly contrived ray, which leaves my other hand free to hold the pistol. You're perhaps aware that the emerald, which lends this lamp its pleasant green color, is very nearly played out, as they say. It's effective in close quarters, but now quite useless over distances. Its power is ebbing even as we speak. Still, it should provide us with some entertaining and edifying sport. I'm quite aware, by the way, that the stone recently delivered to our friend the Peddler might be a fraud. Professor St. Ives wouldn't be so easily persuaded to hand over the genuine article. That's why we esteem the man so highly, is it not? No, sir, I anticipated complications, betrayals, perhaps even opportunities. Now, purely in the interests of science, note the effect of the ray as I increase the power of the lamp."

The Professor's face contorted and twitched more rapidly now. He cried out, gasped heavily, and tried to sit up, although the coffin lid pressed downward on him, and he could do nothing to help himself. His eyes flew open, revealing a look of absolute, unutterable, maniacal terror, and he cried out in a tormented voice, his mad eyes sweeping blankly over my face.

Narbondo's expression, to the contrary, was alive with evident delight, as if he were witnessing a droll scene at the theatre. He licked his lips and narrowed his eyes, nodding his head slightly as if very well satisfied. And yet he was not entirely distracted, for he held the pistol steadily, aimed straight at me.

St. Ives shrieked now, and I could hear his feet hammering against the coffin lid and his teeth clacking together. He looked at me again, and I saw in his eyes, God help me, a flicker of recognition and a silent plea. Without a thought I turned and lunged toward Narbondo, thinking to put an end to his depredations once and for all. There was the shattering sound of the pistol firing, magnified in that small space, and I felt rather than heard myself scream in fear and pure animal loathing.

Chapter 13

Complications and Opportunities

I T TOOK TUBBY AND Uncle Gilbert ten minutes of careful searching to find the cut in the hill where the keeper had alleged that the mouth of the cave was hidden. A dense stand of shrubbery disguised it, but someone had hacked a passage behind it, leading around a corner of rock to the low opening in the hillside. If they hadn't been told where to look, they wouldn't have found it, so completely was it hidden by shrubbery. They stood in the shadows now, taking stock, bushes crowded up against their backs, when they heard a voice coming their way from within the cave—someone apparently singing. They turned hastily and hurried back around the way they'd come, going to ground behind a heap of boulders. The singing—a fine tenor voice—grew louder, and the Peddler himself strode into view, walking jauntily downhill in the direction of the lighthouse like a happy man on holiday.

"Shall we follow him?" Uncle Gilbert whispered. "We can lay him out with the blackthorn, pitch his body off the cliff, and be done with another one of these villains."

"I suspect that he's off to the ransom, Uncle. If we knock him on the head, the greater plan goes awry."

"That's damned unfortunate. His head badly wants crushing."

They watched the Peddler make his way to the cottage, open the door, and step inside. He wouldn't find the keeper at home, for the man had already been hurried off in the direction of Eastbourne with his spare trousers and shirt tied up in a bindle. The keeper's absence might be a suspicious thing, but it couldn't be helped.

They returned to the cave mouth, listened for a moment, and then stepped into the near-darkness across a litter of leaves and sticks.

"No quarter for them," Uncle Gilbert said in a low voice. "That was my old dad's way. He fought at the Battle of the Nile, you know, and don't I wish I could have been there. I'd have knocked a Frenchman or two on the head. Perhaps one of these villains is a damned Frenchman."

"Certainly there'd be more glory in it," Tubby said, not feeling quite so brash as his uncle. He set out, endeavoring to see through the gloom, Uncle Gilbert coming along behind, the two of them walking ever downward into the nether regions of the earth, sometimes in the light of oil lamps, sometimes in darkness.

In due time they saw a brighter light ahead, coming from within what was apparently a room off the passage. There was the scuffling and banging of what sounded like someone laboring over heavy crates, and then two distinct voices, one of which said, "Blast your blasted arm," which was followed by "Bugger off," from the other one. A moment later the bottom corner of a large trunk appeared in the doorway, followed by the wheels of the upright, two-wheeled trolley that it rested upon.

Tubby and Uncle Gilbert stepped back into the shadows, watching as the Tipper himself appeared, pushing the first cart, which held a Saratoga trunk that towered over his head. A second trunk followed, this one pushed by the railway thief, whom Tubby recognized on the instant. He was turned nearly sideways so that the trunk and cart rested against his good arm, like a man shoving open a door with his shoulder. Soon they were out of sight around a bend in the tunnel.

"I say we come upon them from behind while they're discommoded by those trunks," Uncle Gilbert said.

Tubby nodded, but his uncle was already setting out, his statement being more in the line of an order than a suggestion. The two of them crept along like sneak thieves in a dark house. The passage straightened, and there ahead, quite close, stood their prey, the railway thief struggling with his burden, and the Tipper berating him. Tubby glided forward, the blackthorn stick at the ready, which was a good thing, for the Tipper looked back just then, saw him, and gave a shout, which was his undoing. Tubby swung the stick at his head, and the Tipper ducked forward, trying to get out of the way, but he caught the full weight of the club between the shoulder blades. He was driven forward, his forehead rebounding audibly off the corner of the heavy trunk. Uncle Gilbert had waded past Tubby now, his sword cane raised, calling on the railway thief to stand down. The man elected to flee. He hadn't taken three steps, however, before Uncle Gilbert drew back his arm and cast the sword cane like a whirligig at his knees, the weapon whistling as it flew. The man somersaulted forward in a tangle of arms and legs and lay for a surprised instant on his face before trying to rise again. Tubby was too quick for him, and the man found himself looking at the upraised blackthorn. He held up his good arm to fend off the blow.

"It was me that did for your other arm," Tubby said to him, "you crawling piece of filth. Do you deny it?"

"No sir," the man said unhappily, withdrawing his raised arm and tucking it sensibly away under his side. He made no further move to rise.

The Tipper was just then coming round. He stood up, staggered two paces toward the wall of the tunnel, and then collapsed again.

"Come my good fellow," Uncle Gilbert said to the railway thief. "Lend us your one good arm, and we'll let you keep it. Let's have a look inside that Saratoga trunk that our tiny friend was trundling. Jump to it, now."

Puzzled, the man crept to his feet and threw open the lid of the Tipper's trunk, which was filled with carefully stowed bottles of wine, waxed cheeses and cured meats. "Our good luck," Uncle Gilbert said, his eyes greedy. "To the victor go the spoils, eh nephew?" He gestured with his cane. "Stow the lot of it against the wall there, my man. Break so much as a bottle and it'll go rough for you."

He set about unloading the freight, piling it carefully against the wall, until the trunk was empty. The Tipper had come round again. He stood up unsteadily, holding onto the edge of the empty trunk with the look in his eyes of a man about to bolt. Before he had a chance, Uncle Gilbert bent forward and pushed him, and the Tipper toppled over into the trunk with a shout, the lid slamming down over him. Uncle Gilbert sat on it in order to do up the latches and fasten the two heavy leather belts that girt it, and just like that the Tipper found himself lying in the darkness of a locked Saratoga trunk. He continued to shout and to pummel the sides until Tubby whacked on the lid half a dozen times with the blackthorn.

"Now you, mate," Uncle Gilbert said to the railway thief. "That one's yours. I've taken a liking to you, and I give you my warrant that we'll return in due time to set you free—such freedom as you deserve, that is. As for the Tipper here, I have a notion to cold storage him in that room back yonder. It's tolerably dry down here, and he'll stay fresh as a pharaoh for the next century or two."

"You want me to get into the bleeding trunk?" the man said.

"As you value your neck," Uncle Gilbert told him. He unsheathed his sword and took a vicious swing in the man's general direction, and in a trice he was unloading the second trunk, which was filled with much the same sort of delicacies as the first—no doubt intended for Narbondo's larder aboard the submarine.

"In you go, then," Tubby said. "Easy does it." They stood on either side of him, crowding him into it, throwing the lid down and fastening it.

"They'll be tight as bugs here until we return," Uncle Gilbert said loudly, for the sake of the two prisoners. "And if we don't return they'll be dead men." He laughed out loud, claimed happily that he hadn't in his life had such sport as this, and shook Tubby's hand on a job well done.

———⁓———

HASBRO AWAKENED TO find himself bound into a chair— the very same chair that the keeper had been bound into a scant hour earlier, and with the same lengths of curtain line. He quickly found his wits and deduced that his wounds were perhaps more bloody than dangerous, and that the problem lay not in the bullet or possible concussion, but in the infernal device that sat like a toad on the floor some three feet from the chair in which he was tightly secured. It was a simple thing of wires, a clockwork mechanism, and a large bundle of explosives, and it ticked loudly in the quiet room. The face of the heavy clock was imprinted with a grinning moon. Inserted into one of the eyes was a copper peg, which must surely complete an electronic circuit when touched by the minute hand of the clock, which, it seemed to Hasbro, was moving in its revolution surprisingly quickly.

His first wild instinct was to raise the front legs of the chair in an endeavor to hop bodily backward, wanting to distance himself from the device. But although he succeeded, he quickly gave up on the effort, for the device was evidently large enough to blow the cottage and the lighthouse to pieces, and distance would avail him nothing without freedom and an open door.

He struggled now with the bonds, but they were cleverly tied, and his actions simply drew the knots tighter. There was a clasp knife in his pocket—he could feel its weight—but unless he could free either of his hands, it was useless to him. He bucked in the chair, coming down hard on one of the rear legs, which snapped off, tilting him slowly over sideways so that he slammed down onto his side on the floor. If it had been a front leg, it would have freed one of his feet, and he might yet win free, but as it was he could no longer bring any leverage to bear, and his struggles simply propelled the chair in a feeble circle, so that he ended up staring once again at the bomb.

He was weakened, too, by loss of blood or concussion, and it came into his mind that if he lost consciousness he was a dead man. He calmed himself by force of will, moderating his breathing, clearing his mind, and then very carefully he went about the process of testing each of his bonds in turn, distracted all the while by the maddening ticking of the clock, the seconds and minutes slipping away. Freeing a foot would avail him little, and so he attended to his wrists and arms, certain that force would work against him, and that subtlety and patience might prevail.

Time passed, although how much time he couldn't say. He found it necessary to stop more and more often simply to rest, and finally the desire to sleep came over him, subtlety and patience having invited it. His determination had leaked away with his vital fluids, and it was only with the very last vestiges of his consciousness that he heard the door behind him creak open and a gruff voice asking, "What the bloody hell is this now?"

Chapter 14

The Battle
in the Sea Cave

A T THE SAME MOMENT that the gunshot stunned my ears and I threw myself witlessly to the ground, I felt a spray of blown-apart chalk pepper the back of my head, and I realized that the bullet had gone wide, had struck the wall behind me. Narbondo corrected his aim in the heavy, ear-ringing silence that followed, gesturing me to my feet again. He began to utter something, but before the first words were out of his mouth, a shadow filled the doorway, and there stood the Peddler, an evil looking truncheon in his hand, what's sometimes called a "slung shot"—a heavy iron shot with a flexible handle, meant to kill or maim.

"I heard the gunshot, Doctor…" he started to say, and then he saw me standing there, my face still drawn with shock. "Good day to you Mr. Owlesby."

I said nothing. There was scarcely enough space in the small room for another person, and so he remained there in the doorway, digging into his pocket and removing the drawstring bag that he had taken from Hasbro. He handed it across to Narbondo, who fished out the large green stone from within and held it up between his eye and the window. Then he laid it on the table top, picked up a stoppered bottle of some sort of chemical, opened the bottle, and with a glass rod dipped out a droplet of the liquid and touched it to the emerald. A faint wisp of smoke rose from the surface. Narbondo shook his head sadly and swept the emerald onto the floor beneath the table, as if it were worth nothing.

"Mr. Burke," he said, "I suggest that you either don one of the asbestos caps or retire from the scene so that we can continue our experimentation. You've carried out your work admirably, and I thank you for it. I'll make my thanks more tangible in due time, but at the moment I intend to put Busby's interesting device to further tests. Professor St. Ives has made himself a willing subject, and it's time that we put him through his paces, as the quaint saying goes. You might want to adjust your cap, Mr. Owlesby."

The Peddler turned to leave, and in that very moment there was the sound of a heavy thud, and the man was precipitated bodily back into the room, sprawling on the floor, blood flowing copiously from his scalp onto the white chalk. Alice stepped into the doorway now, holding the oak bar from the door. There was cold murder in her eyes. She looked at St. Ives, lying blessedly still now, and then at Doctor Narbondo, who still held the pistol, which apparently meant nothing to her.

There was a long silence as she stared Narbondo down, and I believe that I saw doubt in his eyes for the first time. She reached into a pocket in her waist now and withdrew the fortified emerald, which she had clearly fished it out of the teapot before following me down the cliff, intent upon bringing it to Narbondo herself, choosing to be the one to decide its fate and the fate of her husband.

Narbondo and I stared at the emerald in her open palm, the silence heavy in the room, the world waiting. Then, breaking that almighty silence, there was the sound of a distant, very powerful explosion, and beyond the window I saw a perfect storm of birds flying skyward, and the air was rent with their calling.

"Alas," said Narbondo, shaking his head sadly. "I'm afraid that we've tarried too long with our experiments, and..."

"He's murdered Hasbro," I said to Alice, interrupting him. "They lured him to the lighthouse, locked him in, and detonated an infernal device."

"Of course," she said, her voice steady. "His baseness knows no bounds. It's a Devil's bargain, giving him the stone, and I choose not to bargain with the Devil." And with that she calmly and deliberately flung the fortified emerald, square through the center of the window. It glinted for a green moment in the sunlight and then soared out of sight, bound for the depths of the Channel. Submarine or no submarine, Narbondo would never in life find it.

"Well done!" Narbondo said, affecting his usual bonhomie. But his voice was pitched too high, so that he sounded rattled. He looked down at the Peddler, seeming to notice him for the first time, and he lost himself in a sudden, tearing rage and kicked the man savagely in the back of the head. The pistol shook in his hand, and when he aimed it in my direction, I took a step backward. Narbondo bent at the knees, groping for the cast away emerald beneath the table. He slipped the emerald into his pocket, and then awkwardly picked up Busby's lamp, yanking it loose from its wires, all the while watching us, murder in his eyes.

"Out, you go," he said simply.

Alice dropped her oak club. Narbondo wouldn't give her a chance to use it a second time. He was a careful man, was Narbondo. He had been surprised once, but that would be the end of it. We were at his mercy.

"Downward," he said simply, and I set out down the long steep flight of stairs that led to the moored submarine. I knew but one thing—that I would not allow Alice to board that submarine while I had any life left in me. Soon enough we stepped down onto the boards of the dock. Away to seaward stood the sheer wall of the cavern. There was no sign of an opening of any sort, but seawater was perpetually sucked out from somewhere beneath the wall, and then, after a moment, it swept back in again, the submarine rising and falling on the surge. The entrance to the sea cave, then, lay hidden beneath the surface of the sea.

Narbondo, ever vigilant, fiddled with the latching mechanism on one of the porthole panels on the side of the metal ship, swinging open the panel. I stepped in front of Alice, crowding her back toward the stairs. "See to St. Ives," I whispered.

"Silence!" Narbondo croaked.

But instead of silence there came a growing clamor from above, where Tubby and Gilbert heaved along downward, already halfway to the landing outside the room where St. Ives was held prisoner. From out of that room, as if on cue, staggered the Peddler, truncheon in his hand. Hearing the clatter above him, he turned stupidly and lifted the truncheon as if the mere sight of it would give Tubby pause. But pause wasn't in it for Tubby. Inertia carried him down the last few stairs, and he was swinging the blackthorn even as he came along, cracking the Peddler on the shoulder with twenty stone of moving weight behind the blow.

The Peddler would have been knocked into a cocked hat, if there had been one, but there was not. There was empty air at the edge of that precarious landing. He endeavored to catch himself, wind-milling his arms like a man in a play before toppling over the edge. We watched him fall, shattering himself on the rocks in shallow water, the ocean washing in around him, crabs scuttling away to safety. Tubby stopped just short of the brink and leaned heavily against his stick. But already Uncle Gilbert was rampaging down the stairs, death or glory in his eyes, his sword unsheathed. I saw Narbondo's pistol rise to stop him, and I sprang forward, clipping Narbondo's arm near the elbow. He fell backward with a grunt, the pistol clanging on the metal of the ship and dropping into the dark water. He rolled sideways, back into the vessel, and then sprang to his feet like an ape and reached out to claw at the hatch in order to yank it closed. But he was hindered by Busby's lamp, which he still held on to. He was desperate to salvage it, everything else having gone completely to smash in the last three minutes. It was Alice who sprang forward and snatched if from him, yanking it away viciously. He let out a wild groan, feinted as if to climb out onto the dock again, then slid back into the bowels of the submarine, slamming shut the hatch despite my endeavoring to stop him.

We busied ourselves in trying to find a way in, thinking to haul Narbondo out by his boot heels, but there was nothing to do but hammer on the sides of the submarine as it sank slowly into the dark water with an upsurge of bubbles. There was a humming noise, and lights sprang on within, shining through the portholes and illuminating in the water around it a garden of waving waterweeds and darting fish. Slowly the vessel glided forward and downward, and within moments the lights winked out as it passed from the cavern into the open ocean.

The Last Word

W E RELEASED ST. IVES from bondage straightaway, Alice naturally taking charge. She was solicitous, but left St. Ives his dignity—no fawning over him, only a few tears, her emotion passing away quickly, but enough of it for St. Ives to take heart. You could see the change in his face, the lifting of the clouds that had darkened his sensibilities that distant-seeming night at the Half Toad. Although he managed to accompany us without aid, he obviously knew little of where he was or how he had got there. We trudged tiredly along, Uncle Gilbert regaling us with the tale of the taking of the keeper and of persuading him to give up the location of the hillside cave, and then of persuading the Tipper and his crony to climb into Saratoga trunks, which Uncle Gilbert suggested be trundled down onto the dock now in order to be cast into the sea.

Neither Alice nor I had the heart to say anything about the explosion, although the truth would soon be known—sooner than I anticipated, in fact. The great periscope mirror was of vague interest to St. Ives in his still-fuddled state, although it was of monumental interest to me, for there in plain sight stood the Belle Tout Light and the keeper's cottage, perfectly whole.

The cottage door opened even as we watched, and out walked the keeper himself, looking back and apparently saying something through the open door. He carried a crate full of items that he had apparently looted from the cottage and lighthouse.

"Forsooth!" Uncle Gilbert cried. "The villain returns! We should have burnt his eyes out when the poker was hot! I mean to say..." He glanced at Alice and left off sheepishly.

"I'm persuaded that it's Hasbro's good luck that he *did* return," I said. And it turned out to be true, which we discovered when we followed Tubby and Uncle Gilbert out through the cave into the midday sunlight of the Downs. The keeper, having been ignominiously chased off by our friends, had sneaked back to the cottage to recover a purse of money from beneath a hearthstone. One can only imagine his surprise when he found Hasbro tied into an overturned chair and the infernal device ticking away, getting ready to blow the entire place to flinders. In a desperate effort to save his hidden loot, he had fetched the device out through the open door and hurled it off the cliff, apparently setting off the bomb, which did no more than frighten the sea birds. Then he had prised up the hearthstone, retrieved his purse, filled a crate with odds and ends, bid Hasbro a good day, and went away again.

It was we who untied a grateful Hasbro. Tubby's figurative elephant had been knocked about, but was happily reassembled. St. Ives showed signs of recovery, and so to enliven him further we repaired to the cavern, where we made a brilliant lunch of the would-be contents of Doctor Narbondo's larder, including several bottles of superb wine—I can't recall quite how many. The rest of Narbondo's considerable stores eventually found their way to Uncle Gilbert's house, small payment for services rendered. As for the Tipper and Mr. Goodson, we took them along down to Eastbourne, secure in their Saratoga trunks, where we left them in the care of the authorities.

—◦◦◦—

SEVERAL WEEKS LATER, after Alice and St. Ives had returned from their holiday on Lake Windermere, we revisited the Downs on a balmy, early summer day, only to discover that the hidden entrance to the cavern had collapsed in what appeared to have been an explosion.

Boulders of shattered chalk littered the ground without, and the once-dense shrubbery was blown to leafless, broken sticks. We walked out to the edge of the cliffs, where we discovered that the hand-line down the face of Beachy Head had been cut away as well. Determined to see the adventure through, we made our slow and treacherous descent along the narrow trail, only to discover that the great stone that had sheltered the cleft above the Channel had fallen inward—more likely *drawn* inward, if that were possible—blocking the entrance so effectively that the cavern had become the domain of sea birds and bats and other creatures small enough to find their way in through cracks and crevices. Narbondo had evidently returned to Beachy Head, either to make his fortress secure or to destroy it.

We spent the remainder of the morning scouring the Downs near the copse where we had hidden on that fateful morning, searching for the lens of Narbondo's fabulous periscope. It was a wonderfully sunny day, and yet there was no telltale glint of sunlight on glass. The lens must have had a clear view of the Belle Tout light and the meadow roundabout it, and so must have been in plain sight, and yet it was maddeningly undiscoverable. After a time the idea came into my mind that we must be looking at the lens but not seeing it, the victims of a master illusionist. I was possessed by the uncanny certainty that